A Candlelight Ecstasy Romance®

"THIS SEEMS LIKE OLD TIMES," HE MURMURED INTO HER EAR.

Lee knew he was going to kiss her. She knew she should move, say something to stop him, but she did neither. When his lips covered hers, she braced herself to remain unresponsive. Sensing her resistance, Jake began his assault. His hand at her waist slid down to the base of her spine and pressed her hips against the hard muscles of his thighs. She began to panic as a surge of desire burst in her veins, quickly spreading through her entire being.

"My God, Lee, don't deny me this," he whispered hoarsely.

"No, Jake, darling. Oh, no," she murmured, not caring about anything but the white-hot flame that was consuming her, a flame that only Jake could extinguish. . . .

A CANDLELIGHT ECSTASY ROMANCE ®

A GENTLE WHISPER

Eleanor Woods

A CANDLELIGHT ECSTASY ROMANCE®

Published by
Dell Publishing Co., Inc.
1 Dag Hammarskjold Plaza
New York, New York 10017

Dell ® TM 681510, Dell Publishing Co., Inc.

Candlelight Ecstasy Romance®, 1,203,540, is a registered
trademark of Dell Publishing Co., Inc., New York, New
York.

ISBN: 0-440-12997-4

Printed in the United States of America

First printing—March 1983

To Ell, who never lost faith in me.

To Our Readers:

We have been delighted with your enthusiastic response to Candlelight Ecstasy Romances®, and we thank you for the interest you have shown in this exciting series.

In the upcoming months we will continue to present the distinctive, sensuous love stories you have come to expect only from Ecstasy. We look forward to bringing you many more books from your favorite authors and also the very finest work from new authors of contemporary romantic fiction.

As always, we are striving to present the unique, absorbing love stories that you enjoy most—books that are more than ordinary romance.

Your suggestions and comments are always welcome. Please write to us at the address below.

Sincerely,

The Editors
Candlelight Romances
1 Dag Hammarskjold Plaza
New York, New York 10017

CHAPTER ONE

Lee crouched down behind the tangled frame of what had been a jeep. She reached up with one slim hand and brushed back the tendrils of blond hair that had escaped from the restraining bonds of the narrow yellow band, her hands covering her ears as gunfire once again sounded close behind her. Her blue eyes were tightly closed against the horror that threatened her life.

The sound of running feet caused her to throw a frantic glance over her shoulder. John Matson, a friend and correspondent for an international wire service, slid to the ground beside her in a small cloud of dust. He pushed himself into a sitting position and gave her a lopsided grin. "How's it going, princess?"

"Oh, God, John!" Lee exclaimed in near panic. "What's going to happen to us?"

He reached into the pocket of his khaki-colored fatigue jacket and extracted two cigarettes. After lighting both he gave one to Lee and placed the other one between his lips. "Hopefully the feuding locals will either kill each other or call a temporary truce, granting us enough time to make a quick exit." He exhaled, his eyes squinting against the smoke. "If neither of the before-mentioned solutions materializes, then it's dog eat dog."

"Thanks loads, John," she replied waspishly. "You're wasted as a mere correspondent. You should be in the diplomatic corps. You have such a fantastic knack for placing a person's mind at ease," she remarked acidly.

"I'm sorry, love. I'm afraid I've been around these damn idiots for so long, I've become as cynical as they are." He pulled the brim of the hat he wore down over his eyes against the glare of the sun and then patted her slacks-clad knee in a friendly fashion. "Don't worry, that plane will be here in about thirty minutes. Then we can shake the dust of this damned place off our boots."

Lee cast him a worried look. "Do you really think Ed will be able to land with this going on?" she asked, waving one hand toward the shambles that surrounded them.

"Of course. He's used to it. He can land that crate on a dime. He's also gotten me out of some tight spots before."

At that moment a stray bullet whizzed past Lee's head and lodged in the torn seat of the wrecked vehicle against which they were seeking shelter. She made a move to run, but John grabbed her by the waistband of her slacks and held her down. "Stay put!" he yelled over the rapid gunfire that had broken out again. Lee's blue eyes mirrored the outright fear that held her in its grip, but she forced herself to do as John directed. Never in the twenty-six years of her life had she been so terrified.

In a matter of seconds the noise ceased, and once again only angry shouting could be heard. Lee placed a trembling hand over her mouth, wondering what on earth had possessed her to think she wanted to see the barren beauty of the Middle East!

It had seemed such a fantastic opportunity at first. As a geologist—and supposedly of the weaker sex—the assignment had been a plum. She'd literally begged Simon for the chance.

Simon Garrett, president of Garrett Exploration, had recognized in Lee a certain drive and ambition that he understood. They'd met at a party several years ago, hosted by a mutual friend. During the course of a conversation he learned that she was unhappy with her present employers and their chauvinistic attitude toward women geologists. He'd given Lee his card and told her that if she ever considered changing companies, to give him a ring.

Two weeks later, fed up with a situation that was steadily declining rather than improving, she dug Simon's card from the bottom of her purse and called him. An interview was set up, and in less time than she thought possible, Lee found herself involved in the kind of work she'd dreamed of. Her peers—if not overly enthusiastic at first to find a woman in their midst—placed no obstacles in her path, nor did they delegate the less important jobs to her. In time they came to accept her for what she was, a qualified geologist.

The quest for oil had taken Lee to many exciting places. She'd almost frozen to death in Alaska, had her skin turned a honey color in the hot Texas sun, and was buffeted by a merciless hurricane on the Gulf Coast.

It was a wild and exciting life, and Lee loved it. It had also been the one thing that kept her from losing her sanity during the last six months. Especially when her husband, Jake's, disapproving face forced its way into her thoughts. This last trip to Kuwait had seemed the perfect solution to her personal problems as well as the chance to have a go at a really big job.

When Simon first mentioned the trip and her being included in the group of geologists, Lee had immediately begun researching the country from information in the company files, and bought several books on the area as well. But the authors had failed to inform their readers of the necessity for bulletproof vests. The next time, if there was a next time, Simon wanted something from this godforsaken part of the world, he could damn well take care of it without her help!

Lee looked down at her once sharply creased slacks and her neat wash-and-wear blouse. Both were streaked with dust and grime, complete with a long tear in the fabric on the right leg of her slacks from knee to ankle. There was an angry red welt on her skin beneath the tear that still stung from her encounter with a piece of rusty wire she'd become entangled with in her flight across the courtyard of the hotel. The management had failed to warn her of such hazards, she mused rather hysterically. Dodging wire, stray bullets, and screaming rebels was hardly in her line of accomplishments.

John placed a hand on her shoulder and shook her. "Lee? Are you all right?" he sharply questioned.

She gave a slight shake of her head and closed her eyes for a moment. "I'm okay," she whispered, giving him a weak smile. "I suppose I'm indulging in a bout of self-pity," she confessed rather shamefully.

"And why not?" he responded sympathetically. "It's not every day that you're bounced out of bed by some idiot running down the street tossing grenades about like confetti." He gave her a sheepish grin. "To be quite honest, I was rather astounded myself. After last night's meeting, I thought the hotheads had settled their differences."

"How do you stand this sort of thing, John? Doesn't Patti worry about you?" Lee asked curiously. She'd seen the pictures of his wife and the twins; his voice took on that extra pride

13

of a man truly happy when he spoke of them. Why on earth would he risk it for such an assignment as this?

"If she knew how it really was, she'd probably beat me over the head with a skillet," he said with a grin. "I don't always tell her where I'm going; it's better that way."

"You really love her, don't you?"

"Oh, yes," he answered unashamedly. "She's the greatest thing in my life—besides the boys, of course."

"Then why take this risk?" she asked, unable to comprehend the reasoning for such madness.

He shrugged. "Money's one thing. We want to buy a small newspaper and settle down in some little town and raise the twins. And then I guess there's still a little wildness in me. It's in most men, I suppose—that hankering to take chances." He laughed. "Patti says I should have been born back when the West was being settled. Then I could have had all the 'fun' I wanted."

"Well"—Lee eyed him warily—"I think I've had all the excitement I can stand for a while. If I ever get out of here, I'll never again go farther than fifty miles from my apartment," she declared. "Right now I'm not sure who I'm more angry with, Simon or those . . . those people he's trying to deal with."

John grinned. "Don't feel too badly toward him, Lee. I've been here several times before, and this is the first time anything like this has happened in this particular area. If there'd been

14

the slightest hint of trouble beforehand, he wouldn't have allowed you or the other geologists to come."

"Oh, I know. It's just that I dread all the flap when we get home. If we get home, that is."

"What you're really saying is that you don't want to face Jake, isn't it?" he asked knowingly.

Lee leaned over and fidgeted with the torn leg of her slacks, prolonging her answer. He was right; she was dreading facing Jake. She actually quaked in her boots when she thought of his reaction to this latest peccadillo of hers. "That does head my list of things I'm not looking forward to," she ruefully admitted.

"How long have the two of you been separated?" John asked.

"Six months."

He shook his head. "I still don't understand this bond that exists between you. From what you've told me, the two of you are like oil and water."

Lee smiled at the ridiculous statement. How could she explain that her peculiar estrangement from Jake was a situation that was eating away at her, almost tearing her apart? But that her career, her desire to prove herself, prevented her from making any sort of move toward rectifying the problem. She simply wasn't ready to give up the excitement that came with her job for a life of two o'clock feedings and diapers—not to mention the monotonous routine of keeping house.

"You still love him, don't you?" John softly

15

asked, watching the fleeting play of emotions that came and went in her face.

"Does it show that much?" she asked huskily.

"Only to someone who's also in love." He looked out over the barren sand before going on. "Isn't there a chance that the two of you can get back together?"

"Not in this life," she grimly replied. "I think we've hurt each other so deeply, we can never put the past completely behind us."

Jake's idea of a wife was a woman waiting at home, all soft and feminine, smelling of lilacs and roses, her most pressing problem being what to wear out to dinner or the guest list for her next dinner party. In short, a blinkered, placid cow willing to be led around by the reins of wifely duties and motherhood, the latter seeming uppermost on his list of priorities.

And yet, at variance with these same thoughts of outraged indignation was her deep love for Jake. It was there, and nothing she did could dislodge it.

"Then why put off the obvious? There's something about the finality of a divorce that forces a person to face the inevitable," John reasoned.

Lee shrugged. "I've asked myself that same question a number of times, but I'm no closer to an answer now than before."

Those quiet moments were interrupted by the running approach of Simon Garrett, who was as rumpled and dirty as they were. It was almost comical to witness him in such a state. He was one of the most fastidious people Lee had ever known. The amount of money he spent on his wardrobe was unbelievable.

"Are you all right?" he threw at Lee as he crouched behind their makeshift shelter. Poor Simon. He'd only arrived the day before. At this point his trip could hardly be labeled a success.

"Perfectly." She grinned at him as she watched the rivulets of perspiration streaming down his face. Simon was vain, but nice to work for. He was also one of the few men not intimidated by Jake's wealth. For that she would always be grateful. "It would do loads for my morale, Simon, if you could speed up our departure. I'm afraid I'm not very good at dodging bullets," she added saucily.

Both men chuckled at her calm acceptance of their plight. "Prince Fouadi is still trying to get through to the pilot. He can't land at the local airstrip. The rebels have barricaded themselves in the small office and are threatening to kill anyone attempting to leave. There's an abandoned strip about three miles from here, and that's what he's trying to let the pilot know." He leaned back wearily against the frame of the jeep and closed his eyes. "Let's pray he's successful."

"Amen," John echoed in an undertone.

Lee looked incredulously from one man to the other. "Do you mean to tell me that we have

17

to walk three miles in this heat, with that angry mob at our tails?" she demanded.

Simon opened one eye and glared at her. "Precisely!" he snapped.

"Well, then, I suggest that the two of you get off your duffs and locate some means of transportation," she informed them in a regal fashion. "As you can see, my leg is sore and it's quite painful. I've no intention of hiking."

"And just where would you suggest we look, your majesty? If you so much as stand in the open for five seconds, some sneaky bastard will shoot you! This is a civil uprising, Lee, not a gripe session among housewives. Unfortunately they won't call a truce and allow us to leave." He eyed her as if doubtful of her sanity. "The rebels would love to get their hands on any of us for the ransom. As for you, my addlepated friend, there would be other arrangements made. Do I make myself clear?" he asked in a harassed voice.

Lee had the grace to blush. Suddenly she felt like a child. "Are you implying they would keep me?" she asked in a small voice.

Simon snapped his fingers. "Just like that! With your looks and that blond hair you're at the top of the list. And, I might add, the prince will be glad to see the back of you." At her outraged expression he laughed. "In a way, it's an offhanded compliment. In ordinary circumstances he would enjoy your company enormously. But in light of what's happening, not only does he have the worry of our entire party's safety on his mind, he also has to try and see that you aren't abducted."

Lee quietly digested his little sermon before speaking. "Thank you, Simon. You really have a way of setting one straight." She looked thoughtful for a moment. "Isn't there a better place where we could wait than here?"

"Not really. At least here we have a pretty good view of the square. The others should be joining us in a few minutes. It's imperative that we stay together." Almost before he had finished speaking they were joined by several other geologists and the two young clerks, Susie and Margie.

The men were Lee's coworkers. The women traveled to this small outpost, about fifty miles from town, two days a week to take care of the paperwork. They had jumped at the chance to work the two-year hitch allowed by the company. Any position in the Middle East was immediately snapped up.

Lee had also looked forward to the trip. In the back of her mind had lurked the idea that if she liked it, she would ask Simon about the possibility of a transfer for her. It would give her a chance to put enough miles between herself and Jake so that she wouldn't be forced to see him. Although now it looked as though her idea wasn't such a good one.

The small group huddled behind the wreck for shelter, tensing and ducking instinctively at the intermittent bursts of gunfire. Lee had been floored when Simon, earlier that morning, had knocked on the door of her hotel room and hastily explained the circumstances. Later, when John came for her, she'd gone with him, still frightened but not really believing they were in any sort of imminent danger. After seeing several bodies left in the street and the grotesque expressions on their faces, she no longer doubted!

She'd never considered the question of dying. It had always been something she felt inclined to relegate to her old age. But it suddenly dawned on her that life could indeed be shorter than one realized.

Just then a strange-looking vehicle rounded a corner and sped toward them, screeching to a halt in a cloud of dust beside the small group of people. A uniformed driver, one they all recognized as a soldier in Prince Fouadi's army, scrambled hastily from the cab and informed them that he was to take them to the abandoned airstrip. His message was punctuated with a number of quick glances thrown over his shoulder from the direction in which he had come. There were two other soldiers in the back of the truck, the barrels of their long guns shiny in the glare of the hot sun.

In nothing flat Lee and the other two women were picked up and literally thrown into the cab of the truck. The men scrambled onto the back. After one abortive attempt the driver soon had the truck started and they got under way. By then, Susie, a petite brunette, was wildly sobbing. Lee and Margie were trying to console her, but they too were finding it difficult to calm their own fears.

They'd driven approximately one mile when Lee heard the driver give a startled grunt. She threw him a sharp glance and then looked beyond him. A jeep was speeding across the sand, still some distance from them, the obvious aim being to intercept the truck!

Suddenly the air was filled with bullets whizzing past like mosquitoes at a beach party.

"Oh, please," Susie cried, her face reflecting the fear she felt. "Do something!" she screamed hysterically at the driver and began to pummel him with her small fists.

Lee felt that the situation needed drastic action. She grabbed the frightened girl, pulling her away from the driver, and slapped her a good solid whack on the cheek. Just as she released her hold on Susie, Lee felt a peculiar sensation in her right shoulder. She turned her head to stare at the small crimson spot, watching with fascinated awe as the stain became larger and larger.

"My God!" Margie, the eldest of the three, cried. "You've been shot."

"Yes, I know," Lee responded quite unemotionally and then promptly passed out. Margie caught her unconscious body and shielded her against the unmerciful jolting of the truck as best she could.

Lee regained consciousness enough to be vaguely aware of absolute pandemonium surrounding them. She knew when Simon jerked open the door of the truck and was perfectly aware of the shock that showed in his face. He reached in and took her body in his arms, careful of her wound. "Hang on, honey, we've made the plane. We'll have you to a hospital in no time."

Lee gave him a whimsical grin, her addled brain unable to figure out why his voice was trembling. He was such a good friend, she mused dreamily. The last thing she remembered for several hours was the whir of a camera as a member of John's crew was filming their hurried departure from truck to plane.

When Lee opened her eyes again the first thing she saw was Simon's worried face. She could tell they were still in flight, and there was a terrible pain in her arm and shoulder. "Simon? Are we nearly there?" she murmured, not having the slightest idea of where "where" was, but anxious to reach it just the same.

"Almost to London, honey. We changed planes. The prince placed his private jet at our disposal." He reached for a damp cloth and gently wiped her face. "You'll be in the hospital in a little while, Lee, so don't worry. I think the bullet is still in your shoulder, but I'm not sure. There wasn't a doctor to check you."

She gritted her teeth against the pain. "Were any of the others hurt?" she asked.

"Fred Weems. He picked up a bullet in one leg. But other than a few scrapes and bruises the rest of us are in good shape."

Lee lifted her good arm, her hand grasping

his arm. "Simon, don't let Jake know, please," she begged as the tears began to ease down her face.

"Don't worry about Jake, honey. I can handle him. But don't be surprised if he already knows. He has interests in this area himself, and by now he's probably heard there's been trouble." He shrugged, a look of resignation on his face. "He has spies all over, so you'd better resign yourself to the fact that in all likelihood he'll be in London."

CHAPTER TWO

The sea of faces surrounding Lee and Simon on landing in London came and went. Lee struggled to push back the fog of unconsciousness that engulfed her from time to time, slowly drawing her closer within its grasp.

Simon rode with Lee in the ambulance that had been waiting at Heathrow. During the ride she prayed for the blessed release of oblivion. Perhaps it was her overwrought condition, but the closer they got to the hospital, the more agitated she became.

Finally Simon caught the hand that was twisting and pulling at the blanket covering her and stilled it. "Stop it, Lee," he gently admonished her. He watched her, his gaze shrewd and perceptive. "Jake can't get at you through me, so stop tormenting yourself."

She gave him a look of surprise through pain-filled eyes. "How did you guess?" she whispered.

"You've mentioned his name a couple of times," he explained, failing to tell her that she'd said a great deal more, her love for Jake the main thrust of her incoherent rambling.

Not to be pacified, Lee asked, "Can he cause you trouble?" Jake's power was far-reaching and awesome.

"No. Basically we're in opposite fields of the oil business. I drill for oil, and he supplies the equipment." Simon grinned. "Any fight we have will be out in the open."

"Then you do expect some sort of trouble from Jake because of this?"

"Not trouble in the sense you mean, but he will be mad as hell when he learns of this little fiasco."

"Don't remind me." Lee shuddered. "See if you can bribe the doctors to keep me sedated indefinitely."

Simon chuckled. "Shame on you, Lee. I never knew you were so cowardly."

"I'm not usually, but you've never been on the receiving end of Jake's wrath. He can be quite intimidating."

The last thing she remembered before being whisked to surgery was Simon walking beside her stretcher, a peculiar, fixed smile on his face.

Lee tried to move her right arm from the uncomfortable position it was in, but the slightest effort forced a startled gasp from her lips.

She frowned, and then reached for her injured shoulder with her left hand, only to encounter the bandages that covered a portion of her upper arm and shoulder. Suddenly it all came back to her, the ridiculous flight to the airstrip, her being shot, and the agonizingly long journey by plane.

She shifted slightly, wincing at the thousands of tiny hammers that seemed to be attacking her injured side. She ran the tip of her tongue over dry lips, feeling an almost uncontrollable thirst. A jug of water and a glass were in plain view on the narrow table by her bed, but in her condition she was unable to reach it.

Without thinking she gave way to the tears that she'd been holding back. The combination of self-pity, fear, and a sense of loneliness all came together, reducing her to a sobbing heap. After a few minutes of self-indulgence she dried her eyes on the edge of the sheet, amazed at how much better she felt.

Her thirst, however, remained. So as not to be overcome, she gritted her teeth against the pain and maneuvered her body slowly and carefully toward the edge of the narrow hospital bed. She almost had the jug in her grasp, when the door to her room swung open and in walked Jake!

Lee froze. She was like a puppet whose manipulator had forgotten to pull the string for the next movement. His huge frame seemed to draw the walls of the small room suffocatingly close. Instead of the anger she'd expected there was a tautness etched in the rough features of his face, a grayish tinge around his mouth. The dark hair was rumpled, as though he'd been running his hands through it. He released the door and let it swing shut, and then walked over to stand by the bed.

After satisfying himself that she was truly awake, he correctly read her intentions and poured her a glass of water. One end of a flexible straw was dropped in the glass, the other placed against Lee's dry lips. "Just a sip," Jake cautioned, and removed it when she would have taken more of the liquid. After replacing the glass, he sat on the edge of the bed and simply stared at her for what seemed like an eternity. Lee clenched her fists in an effort not to reach out and touch him. The love she felt for him was slowly destroying her.

"Well, Lee, you really did it this time, didn't you?" He spoke in that low, quiet manner that meant he was only barely controlling himself. "Just what in hell were you doing mixed up in a Middle Eastern fracas?" he threw at her.

Quickly submerged was the warm feeling of love that had surfaced at first seeing him. In its stead grew a slow, burning anger. "Get out of here, Jake!" she exclaimed angrily and turned her head to stare at the opposite wall.

"You'd like that, wouldn't you? Then you could let Simon Garrett take control. Nice, safe Simon. He would never cross you as I did, never put a damper on that impulsive nature of yours. Not to mention the fact that he's several years

27

younger than I am. Is it his youth that appeals to you, Lee?" Jake snarled. He reached over and caught her chin in one strong hand and forced her to look at him. "I'll never allow it, never," he declared in a soft, menacing voice. His hold on her chin eased around to cup her neck in a gentle caress. "How are you really feeling?"

Lee forced herself to speak calmly. "My shoulder is hurting, but I'm sure that's to be expected."

"The doctors assured me it would heal quickly. Fortunately the bullet lodged in the fleshy part of your upper arm, just beneath the skin actually, missing the joint completely. You were very lucky," he stated hoarsely, his dark eyes giving nothing away.

And you're meddling, she longed to shriek, but knew it would be pointless. Jake was a law unto himself, as she'd learned on numerous occasions. From the moment she'd met him at a party given by her sister, Marta, he'd tried to take over her life. Her refusal to allow him to dominate her eventually caused their marriage to break up.

"What brings you to London, Jake?" she innocently asked, knowing the question would annoy him.

"You know damn well what, so don't play the innocent with me. After the news came over the teletype, someone from Garrett's office filled me in on the details and I caught the first available flight."

It suddenly hit Lee just how ridiculous this visit was. Their marriage was over . . . ended. She had definitely decided to file for a divorce. And yet she was still as tied to Jake as when they were living together. It was as though both of them had taken an oath to see which one could hurt the other the most. It had been that way since Lee lost the baby.

She would never forget the stark coldness in his eyes when they allowed him to visit her in her hospital room for a few minutes, nor the silent damnation as he stared at her. The accusation was never actually voiced, but it was there nevertheless.

His actions only added to Lee's own private guilt that she'd destroyed their baby.

She'd been warned by her doctor to take things easy. But the opportunity to go to Texas and conduct a geological survey had been too tempting. Lee felt she had to grasp each chance that came her way, had to prove herself over and over again. Besides, she reasoned, she could rest just as easily in her motel room as in the apartment she shared with Jake. Better, if the truth were known. Their relationship had been anything but pleasant since she learned she was pregnant.

All the resentment had vanished, however, when he'd stood at the foot of her bed and carried on a stilted conversation. Her heart had cried out for him to hold her in his arms and smooth away the pain, the utter desolation she felt. Instead, he hadn't touched her, other than with the terrible coldness that emanated from him.

Perhaps it was this recent close brush with death or the fact that she'd survived without Jake's being there. Whatever, it began to dawn on her that she was no longer dominated by him. She still loved him dearly, but she knew with cold certainty that she could live without him.

Something in her expression caused Jake's eyes to narrow in speculation. He let his gaze freely roam the classical lines of her face, her beauty as delicate and fragile as a rose. Only Jake and her mother knew the iron will hidden beneath the surface.

"You've changed. I wonder who's responsible?" He leaned back on the bed, bracing his body on one arm, his palm outstretched. "Is Garrett your lover?" The steel quality of his voice was colder than the slow drizzle of rain that could be seen from the window of the room.

"What if he is, Jake? How can you have the nerve to question my relationship with Simon when there has been a succession of women for you since we separated?" The look of indifference she shot him bore little resemblance to the pain that was gripping her heart. Her mother took great pleasure in keeping her informed of the different women in Jake's life. Lee often wondered if her mother had been annoyed that he preferred Lee to Marta.

"Then it is true?" he persisted doggedly, and Lee could have bitten her tongue.

She shook her head wearily. "No, Jake. Simon and I aren't lovers, so don't start planning some sort of underhanded revenge to punish him," she told him. "Our relationship is strictly that of employer-employee."

"Oh, it wouldn't be underhanded, Lee. Killing him would be an act I'd find difficult to hide."

She looked at him in surprise, shocked to see that he wasn't kidding in the least. "You're a brute, Jake. But rest assured, when and if I do take a man to my bed, I won't give a flaming damn whether or not you approve. I plan to be free of you as soon as I can get back to the States and file for a divorce," she snapped, her blue eyes smoldering.

Jake leaned over her, one hand on either side of her head. His face was so close to hers she could feel his breath on her cheeks. "You'll never be free of me, honey. Even in death I'll hold on to you," he whispered huskily. With that, he kissed her thoroughly, totally disregarding her injured shoulder.

Lee forced herself to remain impassive to his kiss, hating the traitorous pounding in her chest. Jake raised his head enough to look at her and smiled. He moved his right hand and placed it over her heart. "Your lips tell me one thing, but your heart doesn't agree." He dropped a light kiss on the tip of her nose. "I think I'll follow your heart," he grinned.

"Go to hell, Jake. I'm not interested in taking up the slack in your love life. What's wrong, are you between—er"—she searched for a word to adequately describe the women in his life—"paramours at the moment?" she asked acidly, taking the edge of the sheet and wiping her lips clean of his kiss. She knew the action would infuriate him, and she was correct. The blood drained from his face, leaving it deathly pale. The indomitable thrust of his stubborn chin boded ill for Lee.

His hands closed about her throat, and for one electric moment she was convinced he was going to choke her. "You're very wise to be afraid, my dear. With one snap I could break your beautiful neck. But that would be denying myself something that amuses me, wouldn't it?" His dark gaze raked her unmercifully.

"Have you forgotten that it's only been a few hours since I underwent surgery?" she murmured, her voice shaking even at that much exertion.

The blazing fury in his eyes slowly faded to be replaced by a determined glint that Lee knew well. He moved his hands from her throat and brushed back a curl that had fallen forward across her brow. "Did I hurt you?"

"No, but I'm quite sure the doctor doesn't have that sort of experience in mind for my recuperation," she pointed out dryly.

"Which brings us to the next treat in store for you," he casually replied as he moved from her bed to sit in the chair close by. He reached into his jacket pocket for a cigarette and then withdrew his hand as he glared at the No Smoking sign attached to the wall. "Your doctor has assured me that your injury, while not serious, will necessitate several days' rest. Since I know you won't even consider staying with your mother during this time, I'm taking you home with me until you're on your feet."

Like hell you will, Lee silently fumed. "Thank you for your generous offer, Jake, but I prefer my own place."

"Perhaps you missed something, Lee. I didn't ask you. I'm telling you that you will stay with me until you're well," he informed her in a firm voice, his face imperturbable.

"Jake, I—"

"Save it, honey. By this time tomorrow we'll be on our way."

After his exhausting visit Lee gave a huge sigh of relief. Any sort of encounter with Jake left her feeling battered. But, she thought, it hadn't always been that way.

From the moment they met, there had been some invisible bond between them that grew stronger with each day. And yet she often wondered if part of her attraction had been the fact that her mother found him so objectionable. She loved him, but it had only become obvious to her after she lost their baby. By then she had also lost Jake.

The first mistake she made was in refusing to give up her job. It was silly, she'd argued, to sit alone for days on end while he was out of town on business. Besides, they could have the weekends together. Jake had suggested that she might enjoy traveling with him, but Lee had given him an indignant wave of her hand and bluntly refused. The idea of waiting for him in some lonely hotel room was singularly lacking in appeal.

She let her thoughts go back to the first idyllic weeks of their marriage. At Jake's insistence she'd taken an extra two weeks off from her job. That gave them a month to do nothing but indulge themselves and their appetites for each other.

Jake had been an expert lover—gentle, patient—as he taught her the wonderful mysteries of loving and the giving of her body to him. Unfortunately Lee soon began to experience a tiny niggle of fear that not only did he want to possess her body, but her thoughts, her very soul as well. He was twelve years older than she, and this disparity in age seemed to nag at him. That and her adamant refusal to give up her career.

The last week of the honeymoon, spent in a lovely mountain retreat that Jake owned, saw the first of many arguments that would eventually doom their marriage.

Lee was preparing the trout that Jake had caught that morning, her mind at peace, her body lulled into a state of unbelievable happiness. She heard a sound and looked over her shoulder to see Jake standing in the doorway watching her. For a split second she could have sworn there was a flicker of uncertainty registered in his face, but it was shuttered so quickly she dismissed it, her own happiness blocking out even the slightest hint that Jake wasn't feeling the same as she.

"If you'll set the table, we can eat in about three minutes." She smiled at him before turning back to the sizzling trout.

Lee felt rather than saw him move up behind her, his arms slipping around her, his hands cupping her breasts. "Why wait three minutes?" he murmured, nuzzling the smooth skin of her neck beneath the silken fall of her hair. "I can think of an infinitely more enjoyable main course."

"Oh, no, you don't." She laughed even though her body had melted against his the instant his hands touched her. "I've been slaving over a hot stove, and I demand that you pay proper respect for my labors." She turned in his embrace and slid her arms up to encircle his neck.

"What happened to the insatiable seductress I held in my arms bright and early this morning?" he asked in mock sternness. "The one who plied me with all sorts of sexy promises if I'd only stay in bed?"

Lee tilted her head at an engaging angle. "The unfeeling oaf left me to go play in the water and commune with nature," she said pertly.

"What about the lovely trout the oaf caught while playing and communing?" he teased, his big hands steadily caressing her from shoulder to slender hips in lazy strokes.

"I suppose they're enough of a bribe, but it saddens me to think of a beautiful morning gone to waste," she intoned dramatically, her lips twitching mischievously.

Jake jerked her closer, his mouth swooping to cover hers in a kiss of punishing ecstasy. Lee felt herself weakening, the now familiar light-headedness creeping over her, leaving her clinging to the solid feel of his shoulders beneath her hands.

Suddenly there was a stinging sensation on Lee's arm. She jerked back and grabbed her forearm.

"What's wrong?" Jake asked, concerned, his heavy dark brows drawing together in a straight line above the aquiline thrust of his nose.

Lee grimaced. "Your beautiful trout just popped me," she informed him.

Jake shrugged resignedly. "Remind me never to try and lure you to bed when you're frying trout."

It was while they were washing the dishes that Jake brought up the subject of her career.

"When we get back to Denver there are a couple of houses I want you to see," he informed Lee as he wiped a plate dry and placed it in the cupboard. "Once you give up your job, I know you'll have a lot of time on your hands. Redecorating your own home should be enjoyable."

Lee finished washing the glass she was holding, rinsed it, and then set it in the plastic dishrack. "I thought I'd made myself clear on that point, Jake. I've no intentions of leaving my job."

"Of course you will," he spoke matter-of-factly. "There's no longer any reason for you to storm the citadel of male chauvinism. You've proved that you're capable of performing as well as your male colleagues; now it's time to assume your role as my wife and the mother of my children."

"But I don't want children—at least not for a while." She spoke hurriedly. "Neither do I relish the idea of sitting home all week while you're away. I'd go crazy, Jake." Her blue eyes beseeched him to understand.

"And just where does that leave me?" he snapped, the glint of anger growing as he stared at her.

"Why," Lee shrugged, "as my husband, of course. We'll have the weekends together, plus what other time we can squeeze in."

"Do you want that kind of life, Lee?" he'd asked harshly. "Just weekends, perhaps a night or two in between if we're lucky?"

"Why not?" She tried to sound casual in face of the accusing tone of his voice. All the years of study, of being given the "nothing" jobs flashed before her eyes. She'd reached a certain pinnacle of success in her field, and there was nothing on earth that could induce her to give it up.

37

"How do you plan to work in a baby in this single-minded pursuit of your career you're embroiled in?" he jeered, all pretense at masking his anger gone. He was itching for a fight, and Lee felt helplessly trapped.

"I really haven't given it a great deal of thought, Jake. I suppose when and if I do get pregnant, I'll take a leave of absence." Her gaze dropped before the blazing brown orbs glaring at her. "Do we have to discuss it now?"

"It seems we should have done so months ago," he rasped furiously. He flung down the dishtowel and walked over to stare out the window, his eyes seeing but not appreciating the beauty of the tall aspens in the distance.

Lee got a grip on the quivering that was attacking her insides. She turned and faced him. "I wasn't looking for a man to take over my life, Jake. I thought you knew that. I don't want to be smothered by the boring job of keeping house and having babies. I need more than that from life. Can't you understand? Surely you of all people must know the feeling that comes with success. You've built your own company to the point where it's tops in oil-field equipment. How would you have liked it if someone had told you to stop designing and go become a . . . a bookkeeper?"

"That's a totally ridiculous comparison. First of all, I'm a man," he stiffly informed her. "I hope I need not remind you that you're a woman. As such—"

"As such," she interrupted icily, "I'm supposed to fall in with all your preconceived ideas of a woman's role. Mainly that of being at your beck and call—and having a baby every year. Well, no thanks!" she cried, her anger at his unabashed chauvinism overshadowing her desire to reason with him.

The washing-up was finished in pointed silence, with the evening continuing more of the same. Jake locked himself away in the small room he used as a study, and Lee watched television in the large, comfortable den. The lines of battle were well and truly drawn, with neither side willing to budge an inch. It was a practice that was carried out many times during the stormy two years of their marriage.

Oddly enough, Lee's mother was delighted at their estrangement and lost no time in encouraging her daughter to divorce Jake. Lee had also had two years to view her performance as a wife, and what she saw was not very pretty.

Over the years Lee had become accustomed to fighting her mother. That she was unwanted had been evident for as long as she could remember. Susan Cramer was concerned only with her eldest daughter, Marta, and her career. From infancy Susan had pushed Marta into beauty contests and any other sort of exposure that would further her chances in the field of modeling or acting. Lee often wondered how her sister could allow their mother to dominate her life.

Lee grew up being pushed into the background. It also didn't help matters that the skinny youngster with pigtails developed into a beautiful young woman. She was tall and willowy, with a mane of blond hair that often caused speculation as to whether or not the color was genuine. But her metamorphosis wasn't viewed with favor by her mother.

The rejection had hardened Lee, causing her to withdraw, keeping hidden her true feelings. Jake had gotten closer than anyone, but even with him she was afraid to allow him too close. He was an even stronger individual than Susan Cramer. It was impossible for Lee to see that his feelings for her were simply a show of his love. She had rejected him at every turn without ever being aware of it.

Her bitter recollections were interrupted by the door of her room slowly opening. Simon's head appeared first, and then, seeing that she was awake, he came in. A big grin was plastered on his face. "How are you, honey?" he asked as he walked over and stood by her bed. He took in the bandages visible beneath the sleeve of the hospital gown. "Much pain?"

Lee laughed. "I'm okay. The pain comes and goes. The nurse . . . excuse me . . . the sister, was in earlier and gave me a light sedative. So if I seem a bit balmy, please forgive me."

Simon caught her hand that was lying on the outside of the sheet and squeezed it. "At the moment I can forgive you anything." For the first time Lee got a good look at his face. It looked as though he'd aged ten years. "You really had me worried. I've cursed myself for being every kind of fool in the world for ever letting you go with the survey team. But I honestly had no idea those damn rebels would stage an uprising."

"Don't reproach yourself, Simon. I wouldn't have missed the trip for anything. Although," she grinned, "I could have done without certain phases of their hospitality." She waved to the chair beside her bed. "Sit down and keep me company for a while."

He did as she asked, leaning back with a sigh. "Have you seen Jake?"

"In the flesh," she laughingly replied. "Have you had the pleasure?"

Simon held up one hand. "Please. I haven't been made to feel so guilty since the manager of the drive-in theater shined his flashlight in my car on my first real date!" He shook his head. "Honestly, Lee, he's paranoid where you're concerned. If it's none of my business, tell me to butt out, but just what is the relationship between you two?"

Lee shrugged her uninjured shoulder and lifted her hand in a questioning gesture. "I wish I knew. I'm sorry if he was ugly."

"Think nothing of it," he quickly assured her. "By the way, he said the two of you would be leaving first thing in the morning. Is that what you want?"

"Not really, but at the moment I'm in no position to argue with him. He wants me to stay at his place until my shoulder is better, but there I draw the line."

"Will your mother or sister stay with you?" Simon asked curiously. He was aware of the animosity between her and her family. But surely they wouldn't refuse to help her in light of her present condition.

"I'm afraid that's out of the question, Simon. My mother abhors illness of any sort. Frankly I don't want to be around her for any length of time. We always manage to rub each other the wrong way."

Simon smiled, but he knew that inwardly she was hurting. Personally he considered it quite unnatural for a mother to be so devoted to one daughter and completely disregard the other. He pushed back a cuff and looked at his watch. "I'm afraid I have to rush off, Lee. Is there anything I can get for you before I go?" he asked, rising to his feet.

She shook her head. "Nothing, thanks. Jake's thought of everything." She indicated the toilet articles on the small table and the robe and slippers beside the bed. "There's even an outfit to travel home in."

Simon chuckled. "He doesn't forget anything, does he?" His face sobered as he took in the paleness of her face. "Are you afraid of him, Lee? Because if you are, we can make other arrangements."

"No, I'm not afraid of Jake. Strangely enough, I trust him with my life. It's just that we can't live together," she quietly explained.

"Just one thing, Simon. Save my job," she reminded him.

He leaned down and kissed her cheek. "Honey, you can be chairman of the board if you want it. Just get well soon."

After he'd gone and the sister came in and settled her for the night, Lee let her thoughts return to Jake. She wondered where he was spending the night. Knowing him as she did, he probably had some woman stashed away in London. Women were the same the world over, and he did frequent this part of the globe occasionally.

That unpleasant thought stayed with her until she dozed off. She didn't hear the silent opening of the door or see the tall, broad-shouldered man as he came into her room.

Jake walked over to the bed and listened to her even breathing, assuring himself that she was all right. Next he removed his coat and tie, and slipped off his shoes. The pillow the sister had given him was thrown toward the chair and landed with a soft thud. He turned once again to where Lee lay sleeping, his features unbelievably gentle. One large hand reached out and cupped the side of her face. Still touching her, he leaned down and kissed her fleetingly on the lips. He straightened but remained by the bed, the dim light lending an unhealthy pallor to her lovely face. *Ah, no, baby,* he thought determindly, *I'll not lose you again. What's mine . . . I keep. And you are mine.*

During the night Lee dreamed of Jake.

Dreamed that he was holding her, murmuring soothing words as he had so long ago. His huskily whispered endearments had her replying in kind, her hand caressing his face as she whispered her love for him.

CHAPTER THREE

Lee shifted positions for the third or fourth time in an effort to get comfortable. The pill Jake had given her just prior to their leaving London was wearing off. The throbbing pain in her shoulder had her gritting her teeth as she sought to cope with the discomfort.

"What's wrong, sweetheart? Are you in pain?" Jake suddenly spoke. He'd been engrossed in the contents of a large legal-sized folder for the past hour.

"Some," she readily admitted. The tiny beads of perspiration on her brow caught his eye, as did the clenched fist of her left hand. He stopped a passing stewardess and asked for a glass of water. He then reached into an inside pocket of his jacket for the small vial of tiny white pills. When the stewardess returned he gave Lee one of the pills and held the glass to her lips while she drank. Afterward he covered her with a light blanket and patted her arm.

"Be patient, honey. That pill is dynamite. The last one had you asleep in minutes."

"Thank goodness," she muttered irritably. At the moment she was aching like blazes, not to mention being back in a plane. All she wanted was to be in her own bed with her black tom cat curled up on her pillow. Poor Tom. His nose was always out of joint after one of her trips, but he would really be in a snit this time. The delight of his life was having Lee scratch his head and ears. She looked at her bandaged arm and sighed. One-handed scratching would not please her tom cat.

"Something else bothering you?" Jake asked, looking up from the report he was reading. His briefcase was opened on his lap and Lee could see that it was crammed with work. For a brief moment she wanted to grab the case and fling it through the window of the plane. Anything to rebel against the pain gnawing at her, not to mention the intrusion of Jake in her life.

She gave him a faint smile. "I was thinking of Tom. I don't think he'll be too happy with this." She indicated the bandages.

"Ummm. I suppose not. Who's keeping him for you?"

"Charles. You know I wouldn't dream of leaving him in a boarding kennel."

"Nor would he stay," Jake remarked wryly. "I'll go get him as soon as I get you settled," he told her, and returned to his reading.

"That's something I'd like to talk with you about, Jake. I—"

The cold, icy stare he leveled toward her would have stopped a tank. "Don't say it, Lee," he ground out.

Exasperation showed clearly in her face as she struggled to find words to point out the disadvantages of such an arrangement to them both. "You have quite a—ah—quite a varied social life, Jake. I'd feel like a fifth wheel."

"Just what sort of orgies do you think I indulge in, Lee?" he asked silkily.

She blushed furiously, amazed at herself for being so stupid as to refer to his personal life. Thanks to the press, friends, and her family, she was kept abreast of his comings and goings with disgusting accuracy. She'd considered leaving Denver after their separation, but on giving the matter careful consideration, she decided to remain. After all, there was no need for them to see each other socially unless their friends were unusually heartless.

"Is the answer so bad you can't find words to describe it or are you simply ignoring my question?" he asked, his voice close to her ear.

Lee kept her eyes glued to the back of the seat in front of her, his nearness having a profound effect on her breathing. "Neither, Jake. I was only trying to point out the strain such an arrangement would put on both of us and our guests."

His muttered oath of indifference brought a sting of color to her cheeks. "Do you honestly

47

think I give a royal damn what anyone thinks about the way I run my life?" He leaned over and let his lips rest against her temple for a moment, perfectly aware of the clamor of nerves going on inside her. "I'm sorry, Lee, but my conscience just won't allow me to desert you in your time of need," he assured her, his voice tinged with amusement.

His words so incensed her, she was speechless for several seconds. "Oh! You are a bastard, Jake Rhome," she muttered in an undertone. "I'm perfectly capable of taking care of myself without your interference," she flung at him nastily. "I have friends who are quite willing to come to my aid if I need them."

"Ah, yes," he answered sneeringly. "There's the devoted Simon, Charles, who helps you by keeping your cat, and let's not leave out the dashing Mark Hayman. There are others, but those three seem to be in favor at the moment. However, I'm sure that's only temporary."

Lee closed her eyes against the mockery in his face. "You're not in the least bit funny, Jake. I don't know who your spies are, but you're sadly misinformed. I've only dated Simon a few times. He's a friend, nothing else. So is Charles," she informed him, deliberately leaving Mark's name out.

"And the other?"

"The other?" she innocently asked, pretending an interest in the bandages that covered the upper portion of her right arm and shoulder before turning her head to face him.

"Mark Hayman, damn it. I'm well aware of the rumors floating around about the two of you," he muttered, his mouth twisting cruelly.

Jake sat watching her, a harsh weariness in the lines of his face. Lee felt an urge to reach out and smooth those lines away as she once would have done. But their relationship had altered, leaving her with an emptiness that a hundred Mark Haymans couldn't fill.

"Don't you think he would be an excellent catch?" she asked impishly, not in the least heartened by his display of jealousy. Knowing him as she did, she knew it was simply another of his possessive traits coming to light. If she lived in another city, she was certain she'd never see or hear from Jake again.

"That's something only you can decide. How's he in bed?" he asked, the blunt question taking her by surprise.

Lee shook her head. "I'd forgotten just how outspoken you can be when you're in one of your nastier moods. As to your question, he's a wonderful lover." She leaned her head back against the seat and forced herself to smile. "As soon as our divorce is final you could be hearing wedding bells."

Jake reached for her hand that was lying in her lap. He forced his long fingers between her slim ones and placed their intertwined fingers to his cheek. "You would be a widow fifteen minutes after the ceremony, honey. I'd think about it before doing anything so foolish. There's also the problem of getting rid of the old husband before taking on a new one." With that, he promptly closed his eyes and went to sleep, or pretended to.

The next few hours passed for Lee in a sort of haze. The pill, once it started working, reduced her to a state of acquiescence far different from her usual manner in dealing with Jake. When the plane landed he quickly bundled her into a waiting car and had her installed in his guest room before she could summon the strength to argue. He undressed her in a matter-of-fact fashion, viewing her nakedness with about as much excitement as a surgeon about to operate. After whisking her into a nightgown and settling her in the ridiculously wide bed, he left her alone to go heat her some milk.

While he was out of the room, Lee let her sleepy gaze wander around the familiar setting, remembering the frustrating time she'd had finding the exact shade of carpet to match the tiny blue design in the off-white draperies. Then had come the hassle over the wallpaper in the adjoining bath. All these memories plus the peculiar effects of the medication brought a suspicious brightness to her blue eyes.

She was fighting this back when Jake entered the room, a mug in one hand, her medicine in the other. He came over and sat on the side of the bed, placing the milk on the night table. He turned and stared at Lee, his probing eyes taking in the tears that had escaped and were slowly vanishing into her hairline. He reached out with one large hand and smoothed the dampness away. He'd removed the jacket of his suit and his tie. The once immaculate shirt was now unbuttoned, the cuffs turned back.

The glow from the lamp softened the rough, craggy outline of his face. At the moment his heavy, dark brows were drawn together in a frown as he searched her face. "Is your shoulder aching?" he quietly asked.

Lee shook her head, at a loss to explain. How could she tell him that being in this room, in this apartment, was like having her heart torn from her chest. Living in the same town with him was one thing. But sleeping in the same apartment, and directly across the hall from him, was something else. "I suppose it's delayed shock," she answered evasively, dropping her eyes before his knowing ones.

Jake didn't comment. He slid one arm beneath her shoulders and lifted her—slipping another pillow in back of her. Next he offered her the milk and another of the tiny white pills. "Let's continue with these until you've seen the doctor." He watched her, seeing that she drank all the milk. When she'd finished he took the mug and set it back on the night table.

"What time is it?" she suddenly asked, completely disoriented.

"Eleven thirty," he answered, a smile tugging at the corners of his mouth. He reached out and gently wiped her mouth, his thumb lingering on the fullness of her lips. "You look like a little girl. There's a tiny white line along your upper lip," he teased.

She instinctively reached up to wipe it away, her hand touching his. She jerked back, only to have him catch her hand and hold it. There was a wary glint in his gaze. "You seem unduly nervous. Why?"

Lee ran the tip of her pink tongue over her lips in an unconsciously provocative gesture. "As I said before, I suppose it's the aftereffect of all that's happened. Now that I'm back home and out of danger I feel like I'm about to crack up."

Jake shifted his position so that his left elbow imprisoned her hips between it and his body. He was stretched out, resting his cheek on his hand, in no hurry to leave her. "I don't think that's the problem at all," he told her, smiling. "I think you're afraid to be here alone with me."

Perhaps being in his company for the past twenty-four hours, some of his boldness had rubbed off on her. Although, to be honest, Lee had never been considered timid. Nevertheless, she let her gaze roam over the width of his broad shoulders, the hair-rough chest that she'd so loved to entangle her fingers in. She was always amazed that for such a large man Jake was incredibly lean, without an ounce of superfluous fat on his body. He was simply a giant of a man. But one who could also be infinitely tender.

Stop it! she scolded herself. *You're here to get well, not swoon over Jake.* "Nonsense. Quite frankly I'm not too keen on being here at all.

52

Whether you believe it or not, I do have a decent reputation. But if this gets out, I'm afraid it won't be so decent," she replied crossly, mentally congratulating him on the accuracy of his statement.

The warmth in his dark eyes was immediately gone, to be replaced by cold fury. "I sure as hell wouldn't allow you to go anywhere else, so put that idea out of your mind."

Lee bit back the angry retort that surged forth. Instead, she said, "But that's just it, Jake. You have no right to any say in my life," she pointed out with gentle firmness. "Nor I in yours."

He gave a harsh little laugh. "I've never conformed to the rules of society, honey, as you well know. As for coming to London to get you"—he slowly shook his head—"we were part of each other for a short while, but it was long enough for me to want to protect you. If you had a decent family, I might have reacted differently. As it stands, we're both pretty much alone."

Jake pushed himself upright and came to his feet in one fluid move. After switching off the lamp by her bed he said, "I'll leave both our doors open. If you need anything, just call." He turned on his heels and left the room.

After he'd gone, Lee stared into the darkness. She wouldn't hesitate to hurl insults, fight for her rights, or even demand that he stop interfering in her life. But he was right. They were both alone because of her miscarriage. He blamed her career, her indifference. Deep down, Lee agreed with him.

Suddenly she found herself crying for the loss of her baby, and the lost love of the one man in the world who meant anything to her. She turned her face into the pillow and sobbed. She sobbed for the mistakes—for what might have been and the loneliness that stretched interminably ahead.

Gradually exhaustion gained the upper hand and the slender body was still. The traces of the tears still glinted on the pale face in the dim light. The mass of corn-colored hair was like a soft cloud framing her face.

Jake stood by the bed and gazed down at the tear-ravaged face. The urge to lift her from the bed and carry her to his own was almost overwhelming. His desire for her was greater than he'd ever experienced. The need to possess her, have her back, had become the main priority in his life. For no matter how successful he was in business or how much wealth he accumulated, without her by his side, it simply wasn't worth the effort.

"Enjoy your last days of freedom, my little wild one, for soon you'll feel the gentling hands of restraint once again," he softly murmured. "And for some strange reason, I don't think you'll mind at all."

Lee struggled into a world of wakefulness, her comfortable cocoon shattered by the raised voices that could be heard coming from the living room. She could hear Jake's deep voice speaking in a decisive manner. She stretched her slim body, but was brought up short by the restriction of her sore shoulder. Instead, she settled for flexing her uninjured side, wondering who had dared to incur Jake's wrath so early in the morning.

She threw back the covers and came gingerly to her feet. At first the room spun crazily, but after a moment it righted itself and she made her way to the bathroom.

One look at herself in the large oval mirror over the marble-top vanity caused her to gasp. Her features were pale and pinched, resulting in her looking almost translucent. The wild mane of hair was a nightmare. It was snarled and tangled, as though she'd spent days in the wind without benefit of comb or brush.

She automatically reached for her toothbrush and then stopped, her hand in mid-air. All her toilet articles were neatly arranged on the surface of the vanity, plus several bottles of scent and her favorite dusting powder. A frown of puzzlement marred her smooth forehead as she considered the thoughtful gesture. Either Jake kept a varied supply of cosmetics on hand for his girl friends, or he had pressed Max into service when he'd learned of her accident.

At that ridiculous thought she chuckled. Max was the least likely person she knew to frequent the cosmetic counter of any store. He was a short, stocky man of massive width. At one time he'd been a promising boxer, and still kept his body in perfect shape. His face was a strange mixture of old scars from his days in the ring. But his loyalty to Jake was unquestionable. He'd been down and out when, through some stroke of providence, he did Jake a good turn.

Their friendship had been sealed, and Max had become a permanent fixture in Jake's life. He managed the apartment in Denver as well as the mountain cabin Jake occasionally used. He could also whip up a dinner to tempt the most discerning palate on incredibly short notice. When Lee and Jake married, Max had welcomed her at once, secretly relieved that his boss had had the good sense to choose her. When they parted, he was crushed.

As Lee struggled to brush the tangles from her hair, she promised herself a visit to her hairdresser later in the week. She'd been considering having her hair cut, and this seemed to be the ideal time.

She'd just finished applying a touch of makeup to her face when the door was thrust open. Lee quickly turned, her surprised look encountering Jake's angry one. "What in hell do you think you're doing?" he demanded in an icy voice. He came into the small room and closed the door, leaning his massive bulk against it.

Lee's expression of puzzlement was genuine as she wondered at his strange behavior. "I brushed my teeth, combed my hair, and tried to improve my face just a bit," she smilingly explained.

For a moment she thought her attempt at humor would go unappreciated. But after subjecting her to a brief but thorough scrutiny, Jake gave her a one-sided grin. He ran one large hand over his chin in a gesture Lee knew usually indicated he was nervous. "For a moment I thought you'd slipped out without letting me know." He reached out from his position and caught Lee around the waist and drew her to him. One arm remained at her waist, the other gently cupped her nape. "This seems like old times," he murmured into her ear.

Lee knew he was going to kiss her. She knew she should move, say something to stop him, but she did neither. When his lips covered hers, she braced herself to remain unresponsive. Sensing her resistance, Jake began an assault on her senses that it was impossible for her to remain immune to. The hand at her waist slid down to the base of her spine and pressed her hips against the hard muscles of his thighs, leaving her in no doubt of his complete arousal. She began to panic as a surge of desire burst in her veins, quickly spreading throughout her entire being.

Seemingly of its own volition, her arm lifted to his neck and her fingers tangled in the soft thickness of his hair, her body arching against his. Jake lifted his head for a moment to look into her face, his eyes dulled with _____. "My God, Lee, don't deny me this," _____ hoarsely, his hands caressing her _____

"No, Jake darling, oh, no," sh_____

57

not caring in the least about anything but the white-hot flame that was consuming her and that only Jake could extinguish it.

He slipped an arm beneath her and lifted her in his arms and carried her back to bed. With a tenderness that was so familiar, he slid the straps of her nightgown off her shoulders, baring the proud thrust of her pink-tipped breasts to his smoldering gaze. He supported his weight on one elbow, the other hand cupping one creamy mound as his thumb gently flicked the nipple to a sensitive peak of erection. He leaned down and traced the outline of her lips with the tip of his tongue. "Are you sure you're up to this, honey?" he asked, his mouth now involved in an erotic assault on her ear.

"Oh, yes, Jake, please," she begged. There was no pride left in her where he was concerned. She'd wanted this moment for so long, and now that it was here she couldn't have stopped it if she'd tried. She lifted her hips as he slipped the gown down and off her.

"You're so beautiful, baby, so beautiful," he murmured, his lips paying homage to her body in a way that had her gasping for breath.

Just when she felt she couldn't bear another moment of his deliberate teasing, Jake eased one muscled leg between hers. Lee immediately moved her legs and received him, the softness of her thighs enveloping him within her.

She almost fainted with the shock of the tremors that attacked her as he caressed her, ...ing one nipple slowly between his lips and teeth and then the other, his hands stroking her long, slender legs. Instinctively her hands moved across his strong, taut shoulders, along his firm, muscled thighs, feeling every line, every indentation with her soft fingertips. At her touch Jake reared his head; his eyes closed as he too gave in to the overwhelming passion that held them in its grip.

Lee wasn't sure just how long it was before either of them could move their sated bodies. Jake's head was cradled against her shoulder, one arm laying possessively over her breasts. She turned her head and opened her eyes to meet the indulgent, teasing grin on his face. He lifted one hand and twined a blond curl around his finger, seemingly mesmerized by the color of her hair against the dark tan of his skin. "You're still very quiet when you're making love." He spoke softly, an amused chuckle rumbling in his chest at the color that stained her cheeks.

"Don't tease, Jake," she whispered, pressing her fingers against his lips.

He lifted himself from her and stretched his long length beside her. His arm moved down to rest on the curve of her hip. "I'm not teasing in the usual sense of the word, sweetheart. I'm dead serious," he told her. The dark gaze rested on the slim contours of her face, the small, straight nose and the wide, generous mouth. Her eyes, after making love, were violet-hued, like deep, dark pools. There was also a vulnerability about her that made him want to protect her—guard her against all the disappointments life so often hurled at one. "We have some talking to do, Lee, plus some plans to make."

She met his gaze squarely. "I'd like that. Although I'd like to say you're under no obligation to me just because we made love. We're both adults, Jake. We also know things can get out of hand." Her little speech sounded stilted and cold, but she felt it had to be said. At least she wanted him to know she wasn't trying to slip anything over him. Wanting him was one thing, but entrapment was something else. Also lurking in the nether regions of her mind was her career.

For a moment Jake refused to look at her. When he did, there was a sheepish grin on his face. "I've a confession to make, honey. When I saw the opportunity of bringing you back here, I jumped at it." He smiled. "I'm sure that doctor in London considers me a candidate for the insane asylum. Once he assured me that yours was only a flesh wound, and would heal quickly, I hurried to get you away before you had time to fall in with 'dependable Simon's' plans."

"You mean you've been planning what just happened all along?" she asked incredulously. At his confirming nod she felt some of the happiness leave her. He was so used to manipulating people, one was never certain when he was serious. "Did you also plan each move and word once your plan became successful?" she asked in a resentful voice.

In a flash Jake's hand was beneath her head. He turned it so that she was forced to look at him. "Don't go cold on me, baby. You know it was never better between us than today. If I planned everything, then I must have been a busy fellow when we were married." He shook his head. "Ah, no. I connived to get you back here, but what we've just shared is a complete miracle. I thought it would be weeks before I could entice you into my bed."

Much later, as she relaxed in a warm bath, the unbelievable tender moments she and Jake had shared were somewhat marred by his admission that he'd deliberately planned the entire thing. Not that she was really surprised, but it did cause her to wonder just why he'd gone to such great lengths to get her alone. She mentally ticked off the obvious reasons and came to the conclusion that he must be feeling the hot breath of pursuit breathing down his neck in the person of Sharon Trappe, the latest in a succession of women in his life.

Oh, well, she reasoned as she soaped one shapely leg, at least he'd received some compensation for the brief interruption she'd caused in his life. And, her conscience prodded her, so have you.

Max prepared a breakfast for Lee suited for a king. He fretted and fussed like a mother hen, pressing her to try a little of this, a little of that. Finally Lee raised her hand in self-defense, saying laughingly, "Please, Max. I can't possible eat another bite."

His crestfallen expression reminded Lee of a small boy being refused a toy he particularly wanted. He ran one ham of a hand over his chin. "Jake won't like it, honey. He gave me my orders. I'm to put some weight on you. Although"—his misshapen face broke into a grin—"I think you're just right the way you are."

"Thank you, Max. And you can rest your mind, I've no intentions of gaining an ounce simply to appease Jake. Besides"—she grinned wickedly—"at the moment I think he's got enough problems on his hands with Sharon Trappe without concerning himself with my physical condition."

Max chuckled. "The lady does seem to be a bit anxious." He took a sip of coffee. "But I don't think she'll get very far. The boss is too smart to be taken in by the likes of her."

"Stranger things have happened, Max. After all, Jake's not getting any younger. For that matter, neither am I," she remarked ruefully.

Max studied the dark brew in his cup for several seconds before speaking. "It's frustrating to watch two people you care for trying to destroy each other," he remarked gently.

Lee didn't comment, knowing full well to whom he was referring. She knew he was hoping that by staying at the apartment she and Jake could rekindle the love they'd once shared. But how could she explain to him that her love for Jake hadn't surfaced until his had died—if it had ever lived, that is. That his insatiable determination to change her and her inability to share her life with anyone had left them both scarred and wary.

CHAPTER FOUR

The doctor came and went, declaring Lee's condition to be improving. His only instructions were that she not use her arm excessively for a few more days and to get plenty of rest. The stitches were due to come out soon, and he would tell her more at that time.

After seeing him to the door, Lee returned to the living room. She dropped to the sofa next to Tom and scratched his ears in an absentminded fashion. If the doctor's opinion was anything to go by, there was no real need for her to remain here. "So, my spoiled friend, you made the trip for nothing," she told the big black cat. He blinked sleepily at her, his steady purr loud against the silence of the room.

She let her head rest on the back of the sofa as her gaze slowly passed over the comfortable room. There'd been little to do in here, she remembered, just the addition of a couple of chairs, a lamp, and a print by an artist friend of Jake's.

At least he hadn't attempted to expurgate her presence by banishing her decorating efforts to the attic, she reflected moodily. Of course that could be viewed from two different angles, she reasoned, tending to lean toward the idea that he wouldn't have given a damn if she'd staked out a buffalo in the middle of the room!

It suddenly struck her that even with her poor contribution to their marriage, Jake hadn't been an ideal husband. His indifference toward her decision to continue working after her miscarriage was one clear indication that he hadn't had the time or the inclination to get her to change her mind. Seeing him in action since then left little doubt in her mind that his indifference was as equally destructive as her own behavior.

The ringing of the doorbell sounded in the background. Lee was so engrossed in the mental gyrations of sorting out Jake's latest move, she paid it no heed. Thus the entrance of Sharon Trappe caught her completely by surprise.

The petite brunette erupted into the room as though jet propelled, with Max in hot pursuit!

She came to a stop in front of the sofa, her green eyes running over Lee as though she expected to see a toothless hag of questionable mentality. The slight quivering of her small nose left no doubt as to her displeasure at finding Jake's wife ensconced in his apartment.

65

Lee's hackles immediately rose at the outright rudeness of the woman—with *woman* being the key word. She would never see thirty again! Lee deliberately turned to Max and smiled. "Thank you, Max. I'll take care of our guest." She then leveled her most insolent gaze toward the intruder, letting it slowly move from the long hair—too long for her age—down the expensive lines of the blue suit, on to the small feet in the taupe-colored pumps.

Under this scathing appraisal the woman bristled like a small cat, her thin lips drawn in a straight line of disapproval. "So, you're the former Mrs. Rhome." She spoke in her most condescending tone, stressing the word *former*.

"No, I'm the present Mrs. Rhome. But I'm afraid you have me at a disadvantage. Just who are you?" Lee replied smoothly. "Jake and I've been so busy, he didn't tell me to expect a visit from anyone today."

For a moment Lee thought the woman would explode. She opened her mouth several times in rapid succession. Finally she said, "I'm Sharon Trappe," as though the name should immediately put Lee in her place. "I'm quite used to dropping in on Jake at odd hours. There's no need to disturb yourself, my dear. I'm at home here, I assure you," she replied cattily. She walked over and sat down in one of the lovely blue overstuffed chairs that Lee had added to the furnishings of the room. She leaned back and demurely crossed her ankles, as if waiting for Lee to leave. "Tell me, Miss, er,

I'm sorry, but I really don't know what to call you," she continued in the same condescending manner.

For a moment Lee was tempted to call *her* something, but decided against it. "Why don't you try Mrs. Rhome? It is my name, and I really don't think we're likely to become friendly enough to establish a first-name basis."

"Tell me, Mrs. Rhome, just what did you mean when you said you and Jake had been busy?" She arched her thin brows. "I'm not sure what kind of game you're playing, but I happen to know that Jake had to cancel our plans to buy my engagement ring to fly to London." She imparted that bit of information importantly.

"I know."

This had the desired effect and Lee mentally congratulated herself on the small victory.

"You know?" the other asked incredulously.

"Yes. About him going to London, that is, not the part about buying a ring. He came to London to get me," Lee told her, almost smiling at the raging fury that rushed to the green eyes. "I was involved in an accident and"—she gave an indulgent lift of her shoulders—"Jake, being Jake, rushed right over."

Several seconds went by before Sharon was able to speak. Her face went from an alarming shade of white to red. Her bosom heaved with suppressed anger. "You're lying!" she lashed out in a shrill voice. "Besides, you don't look like you're ill to me, so just what game are you playing?"

"No game. But please yourself and ask Jake. Perhaps you'll believe him," Lee answered. She moved Tom from her lap to the cushion beside her and then rose to her feet. "I'm sorry, Miss Trappe, but I must ask you to leave. I have several appointments and I'm running a bit late." She couldn't resist a final jab. "If you have some message for Jake, I'll be happy to relay it for you."

Sharon had no recourse but to give in to Lee's cool dismissal. She did so with ill grace, obviously not pleased at being placed at such a disadvantage. "I'm perfectly capable of seeing that Jake gets my messages. And you can rest assured he'll hear exactly what I think of this ridiculous charade. You're obviously taking advantage of his generosity."

"Dear me," Lee murmured in mock regret. "I'm afraid you don't know Jake very well. He never does anything without a reason." She gave Sharon a deliberately pitying look. "Perhaps he's trying to tell you something."

After glaring angrily at Lee, Sharon turned on her heels and rushed from the room, leaving behind the heavy scent of her expensive perfume.

Lee was still for several moments after her guest departed. Apparently Jake had used her accident as an excuse to escape Sharon's clutches. She wandered aimlessly about the room, her heart not wanting to accept what her mind projected so forcefully.

In a sense she really wasn't surprised. Jake had always been a law unto himself. But it was the first time she'd been on the receiving end of one of his schemes. It was a bitter pill to swallow. At least it reaffirmed her original plans— to remove herself from Jake's control as speedily as possible.

The remainder of the day passed in relative calm. Lee was surprised by a visit from her sister in the late afternoon, and at the fact that Jake had called Marta when he learned of Lee's accident. Lee managed to conceal her surprise, and found herself actually enjoying Marta's company, finding her to be a very interesting person away from the domination of their mother. It suddenly struck Lee, as they talked, that thanks to Susan Cramer, the two sisters were virtually strangers.

So when Lee asked Marta if she would come back the next morning and help her get settled in her own apartment, she was surprised by Marta's unhesitating yes. "But, please, don't tell Mother I asked you, Marta. I'm sure it would only cause more dissension between us," Lee bluntly reminded her.

"I'll help you on one condition," Marta announced with a twinkle in her eyes.

"Let's have it," Lee answered curiously. She hadn't seen such sparkle and animation emanating from her sister since Marta landed her first modeling job.

69

Marta, now that she had Lee's full attention, seemed to lose some of her self-confidence. She fidgeted nervously with the coffee tray Max had brought them earlier before speaking. "I've been seeing someone for several months now, and Mother knows nothing about him," she hurriedly confessed.

For one incredible moment Lee was tempted to laugh. But on closer observation she could see that Marta wasn't kidding in the least. It was obvious that such an admission—not to mention the act itself—had taken enormous courage. "I think that's wonderful," she said enthusiastically. "I'm only surprised that you've allowed Mother to run your life for as long as she has."

Marta leaned her head back against the high back of the chair and briefly closed her eyes. "I know." She gave Lee a look of regret. "She'd been managing my life for so long, I'd almost forgotten that it is my life. That's one thing I always admired about you, Lee. You defied Mother from age one."

"You really think so?" She shook her head. "Funny, but I've always felt left out by the two of you. When I was younger it really hurt. But over the years I've grown so accustomed to it that it's made me rather independent." She grinned wryly.

"I'm positive you've always intimidated Mother. She's never known exactly what to do with you."

"That's funny," said Lee. "The only thing I

ever really wanted from her was love. But I accepted long ago that she and I would never be close. We're either poles apart or too much alike. Perhaps I remind her of Dad—and you know what their relationship was like."

After Marta's visit Lee enjoyed a quiet dinner with only Max for company. Jake had called earlier, while she was napping, informing them of a change in his plans. He'd be out of town for a couple of days. This information was met with a sigh of relief from Lee. She wasn't ready for a confrontation with him. Resentment flared in her at being the goat in his scheming against Sharon. Knowing him as she did, it made sense to her that his feelings for the woman must run deeper than he was ready to admit. *That would account for his hurried flight to London on the pretext of rescuing me,* she thought gloomily. He needed time to consider such a serious step as marriage to Sharon.

The next morning, after much protesting from Max, Lee, with Marta's help, finally returned to her own place. Afterward she felt as limp as a noodle. Seeing the pinched look about Lee's mouth, Marta offered to fix lunch, which Lee quickly accepted.

While they ate the sandwich and salad, Marta said, "Forgive me for being nosy, Lee, but did I detect a certain uneasiness in you, being at Jake's place?"

Lee considered the question before answering. "Yes. I don't like being used," she muttered, stabbing a piece of lettuce in her salad

71

bowl as if it were the man in question. "It seems that somewhere in the back of my dear husband's mind lurks the brilliant idea that I'm the perfect foil against the various women in his life."

Marta chuckled, her lovely face sympathizing with Lee, but amused all the same. "Somehow I don't see Jake as the sort to need anyone's help in getting rid of a woman, honey."

"But that's just the point, Marta. I don't think he wants to get rid of Sharon Trappe. According to her they were ready to select her engagement ring when Jake left for London."

"I think he was genuinely upset when he heard of your accident. At least he sounded that way when I talked with him," Marta assured her. "And by the way, I would have come with him, but he insisted there was no need."

"Thanks. I'll admit there were times when I didn't hear from you or Mother when I did indulge in a bout of self-pity."

"Well, at least the accident has served to break down the wall between us. As for Mother"—Marta shrugged—"who knows? When Jim and I tell her our plans she just might have a nervous breakdown."

"Nonsense," Lee replied briskly. "Once you stand her down and refuse to let her run your life, she'll bounce back. Oh, she'll do a number on you, how she's sacrificed everything for you, the works. But don't be fooled by her, she's enjoyed every minute of it. In the end she'll come around."

"You sound like Jim. He resents us not telling her our plans now. Poor Mother. She seems doomed to have strong-willed sons-in-law."

Lee laughed. "It must be frustrating. At first she seemed so happy with Jake, or rather with his bank balance, I'm not sure which. But when she ran up against his stubborn will, he immediately became a monster."

After washing the few dishes they'd used and making sure that Lee was settled in, Marta left. Lee closed the door after her, grateful for her help, but glad also to find herself alone.

The first thing on her agenda was a nap. The doctor had urged her to get plenty of rest. And though she had used her arm only slightly, it and her shoulder were burning and throbbing, although her physical pain was nothing compared to the emotional pain she was suffering. Even while she'd been with Marta one part of her mind had remained cordoned off, taken up entirely with Jake and the underhanded trick he'd pulled. Somehow, in an illogical way of thinking, it also gave her a small sense of satisfaction at having caught him—or so she thought—in a compromising situation.

After a nap and a nice long soak in a warm tub, Lee's perspective had altered slightly. She lectured herself regarding Jake and vowed to get over the love she felt for him if it killed her. *Don't be such a nerd,* her conscious scoffed. *You haven't got what it takes to play the fair maiden slowly wasting away from the disappointments of lost love!* That ridiculous picture brought a smile to her lips in spite of her slightly down attitude.

The tall man, his muscular build at variance with his profession, handed Lee a large oval hand mirror and stepped back. "I hope it pleases you," he announced stiffly. She couldn't help but grin at his spiteful tone. Fred, as unlikely a name for a hairdresser as any she had yet to hear, had snipped and shaped her hair from its shoulder length to the riot of golden curls that now covered her head. He'd been appalled at her request, and had only given in when she'd threatened to go to someone else.

Lee approvingly viewed his handiwork from every angle. "I love it, Fred," she cried in an excited voice. "I can't imagine why I haven't had this done sooner."

"Quite possibly because up and until today you were a sane individual," he muttered disgustedly.

Not to be influenced by his rather dour opinion, Lee quickly paid his receptionist and left. Once outside in the cool autumn weather she felt much the same as a sheep without its wool. But regardless of the naked sensation, she was determined to keep her hair short. It was just one of the many things she planned to do over the coming weeks to help purge her mind of Jake. The exorcism would be painful, but she was determined.

Lee hailed a cab and gave the driver the address of her office. There'd been no word from Simon since her return, and she was fairly certain she knew why.

Her entrance into the offices that housed Garrett Exploration ranged from affectionate hugs from all to gasps of dismay at her shorn locks. Upon hearing the commotion brought about by her visit, the door to Simon's private office was thrust open and the boss himself stood viewing the laughing group with a frown.

"Miss Jones!" he yelled over the noise of the melee. "Have I missed something?" he asked sarcastically. "Some holiday perhaps?"

Brenda Jones, his receptionist, jumped a foot, her attractive face turning several shades of red before settling on a deep crimson. She was topnotch in efficiency, but was so in awe of Simon it was pathetic. "Er . . . er, I—I'm sorry, Mr.—"

"Dear Simon," Lee cut off the girl's stammering voice. "Grouchy as usual." She grinned, making her way toward him.

"My God! What have you done to your hair?" he asked disbelievingly, eyeing her new hairdo as though he expected an egg to drop from it.

Lee's lips twitched at his shocked reaction, knowing Jake's would be ten times worse. "I had it cut, you silly goose. It was too much to handle with my sore arm."

Simon recovered enough to grab her by the elbow and hurry her along to his office. Once there, he closed the door on the startled faces of his staff and turned to Lee. "Are you out of your mind? You're supposed to be resting."

"I did rest. The doctor said to get at least an hour-long nap each day and not use my arm excessively." She shrugged. "Other than that, it's business as usual."

Simon's forehead creased as he listened to her. "That's not what Jake said," he insisted stubbornly.

"Oh? Just what did the great lover of all time have to say on the matter?" she asked frostily as she seated herself in the comfortable armchair at one end of the desk.

Simon walked around to his chair and sat down, one hand rubbing his chin in thoughtful meditation. "Jake, the fire-eater, informed me yesterday that the doctor had ordered complete bed rest for at least two weeks. That he'd found you to be in a state of near exhaustion."

Lee didn't speak immediately. At the moment her mind was taken up with hurling every oath she'd ever learned, and a few of her own, at the mocking image of her tormentor. "He's a louse," she fumed. "He wasn't even there when the doctor arrived. As a matter of fact, I haven't seen Jake since yesterday morning. I moved back to my apartment today."

"I see," Simon murmured, taking note of the flushed cheeks and the fire in Lee's blue eyes. "Does he know about the new look you've given yourself?" he asked, gesturing with one hand toward her hair.

Lee grinned. "No. And I can hardly wait for him to see it. It should really set him off."

Simon shook his head. "How can the two of you stand this constant bickering? Hasn't it ever occurred to either of you that if you'd put as much time and effort into getting along with each other, you might be surprised by the outcome?"

"Don't be ridiculous, Simon. Of course I have," she retorted indignantly. "But there are things about our relationship that are unique. Simple logic doesn't seem to apply. And anyway, at the moment Jake is, I think, about to be caught by his latest girl friend, Sharon Trappe."

"My God! How did he ever get tangled up with her?"

"Do you know the lady?" she asked mischievously, chuckling at the scowl that covered his face.

"Sort of," he murmured evasively.

"Sort of?" Lee persisted. "That's the same as saying yes, but mind your own business. Come on, Simon, give."

He grinned sheepishly at her. "She's been divorced for several years. Apparently she's looking for another wealthy husband." He threw out those two facts grudgingly.

"Is that all?"

"She was married to a good friend of mine. She's also the spoiled and selfish daughter of Thomas Trappe, the industrialist. If she's got her hooks into Jake, he'll find it difficult to shake her off."

"Oh, I wouldn't count on that. I've a feeling she's met her match in him. Although I do resent him using me as his scapegoat," she remarked bitterly.

Simon leaned back in his heavy chair and smiled. "Are you jealous or is it just plain orneriness?"

She chewed at her bottom lip, her eyes revealing more than she was aware of. "Both."

"Then why in hell don't you go after him?" he asked incredulously.

Lee reached into her handbag for one of the cigarettes she smoked occasionally. Simon leaned across the desk and lit the tip with his lighter. She came to her feet and wandered about the large, comfortably furnished office. The well-appointed room reflected the man, she thought fondly. And why couldn't she care for that same man, she'd asked herself hundreds of times. But she knew the answer. There was no great mystery about it. Jake was in her bloodstream like some potent drug. Their impromptu clashes worked as a fix whether she cared to admit it or not.

She turned and looked at Simon, who had been patiently observing her perambulation about the office. "I suppose it's pride. Or it could be fear of rejection." She lifted her hands in an expressive gesture. "If I were smart, I'd get out of this town for good."

"I don't agree," he remarked. "That would only submerge your feelings for him. Why not become seriously involved with another man?

There's nothing like a good romance to shake the cobwebs loose. Like Mark Hayman, for instance."

She stubbed out the remains of her cigarette and reached for her handbag. "I'll think about it." She started toward the door and then turned. "By the way, do I still have a job?" She phrased the question to appear light and teasing, but inwardly she was uneasy.

Simon saw through the smoke screen and nodded. "You most certainly do," he emphatically declared.

"Thanks, Simon—for everything," she added, and waved good-bye.

The remainder of the day passed without incident. After leaving the office, Lee did a bit of shopping and then went home. She fixed a sandwich and glass of milk for supper and then went to bed, armed with two new mysteries she'd bought.

It was close to midnight and Lee had just gotten to the really interesting part of one of the paperbacks she was reading. The heroine was being chased by a man with a horribly scarred face. The skin on Lee's neck tingled as she became engrossed in the story. The young woman slipped in her effort to escape and fell, the looming shadow of her pursuer coming closer and closer. She opened her mouth to scream as two heavy hands gripped her shoulders.

Suddenly Lee sat bolt upright, the book sliding from her startled hands as a thunderous banging threatened to loosen the front door of her apartment from its hinges. Even Tom reacted to the frightening noise by springing to his feet and arching his back, his tail resembling a bottle brush.

Lee reached for the robe on the foot of the bed, shrugging her arms into it as she hurried to investigate the annoying intrusion, and to give whoever it was a piece of her mind.

CHAPTER FIVE

Lee grasped the handle to fling open the door, but then thought better of it. After all, it could be someone mistaking her apartment for another—some prankster. She made sure the safety chain was in place and then in a cross voice asked, "Who's there?"

"Open this damn door, Lee, and be quick about it," came the angry command from Jake.

She jumped back at the sound of his voice, momentarily startled out of her unpleasant mood. She looked frantically about the darkened living room as though expecting some solution to appear out of thin air. When that didn't happen she shrugged her slim shoulders and muttered, "What the hell. If I don't let him in, all the neighbors will witness our fight." She reached out for the chain and released it and then opened the door. Quickly stepping back, she switched on a lamp.

Jake stood with a hand on either side of the doorframe, a menacing scowl on his face. His dark eyes resembled tips of steel as they raked her in quick appraisal.

"Well?" she threw at him to cover her own nervousness. "After disturbing the entire building, are you going to remain standing there all night?"

He pushed his large body away from its leaning position and walked into the living room. It was the first time he'd been in the apartment. His gaze quickly touched on his surroundings, an ecletic blend of personal and professional touches that culminated in a very comfortable and pleasant room.

During his brief but thorough examination— his gaze lingering on the light coming from her opened bedroom door—Lee waited with resigned patience. She kept her clenched fists jammed in the pockets of her robe, determined not to fidget. Hopefully, if she could avoid an outright fight with Jake, he'd leave once he knew she was all right.

She moved from her position by the door and walked over and sat down in one of the matching floral print chairs facing the sofa. She leaned back, seeming completely at ease. "Would you care for a drink?" she asked, more to break the strained silence than actually being hospitable.

Instead of the outburst she was dreading, Jake surprised her by accepting. She got up to fix his usual Scotch and water without even thinking. When she returned from the kitchen she viewed with raised eyebrows Jake's form, comfortably sprawled on her sofa, his eyes closed. His jacket and tie had been carelessly thrown toward a chair—one sleeve trailing on the carpeted floor.

Lee set the drink on the low table in front of the sofa within easy reach, and then returned to her chair. Again she steeled her features to reveal nothing of the turmoil going on inside her. She was well aware of the emotional battle going on in the room, but unsure of the outcome.

"Why did you leave my apartment when I specifically told you not to?" he asked after a seemingly interminable length of time had passed. He pushed himself up on one elbow and reached for the drink. After taking a sip he turned back to Lee. "Has the cat suddenly got your tongue?" he asked mockingly. The glow from the one lamp left part of his face in shadow, the contour and angles of his tanned face taking on a faintly menacing look.

"I found it a trifle crowded." She propped an elbow on one arm of her chair and rested her chin in her hand. "Besides, I've never cared to be part of a harem," she informed him innocently.

Jake downed the remainder of his drink and banged the glass down on the table. "What the hell are you getting at? What harem?"

Lee tilted her head to one side, a small frown

marring her smooth forehead. "Perhaps harem isn't the proper word. But I do resent you making love to me while your fiancée waits in the wings, so to speak. Miss Trappe was rather upset at finding me in your apartment."

A brief smile flashed across his face. "What's wrong, honey, are you jealous?" he taunted.

"No," she calmly answered, clamping a tight rein on the rush of cutting remarks that hovered just beneath the surface. "I think disgust better defines how I feel. Especially when the future Mrs. Rhome is shopping for her wedding dress."

"Leave Sharon to me, Lee. There's no reason for you to concern yourself with her."

Lee stared at him in stunned disbelief. "Are you serious?" She gave a short, mirthless laugh. "I don't believe I'm hearing properly. You make love to one woman without the slightest regard for another you've asked to be your wife."

"Just for the record, I have not asked Sharon or anyone else to marry me," he said in a terse, clipped voice.

"Well, I hate to be the bearer of bad news, but the lady certainly thinks you did. She took great delight in telling me that she was shopping for an engagement ring and that the two of you were sleeping together." Why had she added that last part? she asked herself. For whether the woman's insinuations were true or not, even the thought of them making love was painful.

Jake pushed himself upright and then stood up. He ran one hand across the back of his neck and wearily flexed his broad shoulders. "I'm afraid she imparted several bits of information hoping to cause trouble." He began to prowl about the room in a restless fashion. "I'll admit I've not led a celibate existence since our separation, but Sharon Trappe was never my lover." He came to a stop directly in front of Lee. Leaning down, he placed a hand on each arm of the chair, his face only inches from hers. "Is that really why you left?" he asked huskily.

Lee felt compelled to meet his knowing gaze. She also noticed for the first time the tired lines etched in his face. "Partly," she murmured.

"And the other?" he prodded.

"I wanted to be away from your influence," she answered unhesitatingly.

"So you admit that I do still have some effect on you, huh?"

"I don't think there's ever been a question of either of us being immune to the other, Jake. But we've also hurt each other terribly," she reminded him.

Obviously not pleased with her answer, he straightened and then walked back to take his former position on the sofa. "We could always have another go at it," he remarked offhandedly, his sharp gaze never leaving her face.

"But what about love, Jake? Does that figure in this hypothetical arrangement? Sex is great, I'm all for it. But not simply as a means of physical release."

"Am I to conclude from that remark that you're in love with Hayman?" he asked nastily.

"Is that so unreasonable? At least with him I don't feel I'm being used as a buffer against half the women in Denver," she lashed out.

"You'll never have him, Lee. I'll see to that," he reminded her in a deceptively smooth voice. "By the way, I like your hair. Although I'd rather you didn't cut it again. But I'm sure you only did it because of your accident," he remarked with a perfectly straight face, ignoring the light of battle that sprung so readily to her eyes.

Lee felt like slapping him. He knew damn well part of the reason she'd had it cut was to get at him. Her hair had always been a special thing to Jake. When they made love, he'd bury his face in it, his fingers running through it as if fascinated by it. His calm acceptance only incensed her. She got up and walked over to a small rosewood desk where she'd left her cigarettes. She removed one and lit it. "I'm glad you like it, Jake. I'm thinking of keeping it this way. It's so easy to care for," she replied in a cool voice. When he didn't answer, Lee cast a wary glance over her shoulder. The sight of Jake sound asleep did little to appease her ruffled feathers.

She moved quietly over to him and stared at him for a moment, his breathing deep and relaxed. The urge to reach out and touch him was almost overwhelming. The harsh lines of fatigue she'd noticed earlier were less severe as he slept. The sensuous curve of his lips only moments ago had been drawn in a thin, disapproving line. But in spite of the unguarded pose of sleep, there seemed to be new lines added to the tiny crisscrosses at the corners of his eyes. All these thoughts crowded Lee's mind as she stared down at him.

Why, Jake? Why? she silently cried out. *How did we manage to completely ruin any chance at happiness with each other?* There was an imperceptible shake of her head and a smothered sigh of regret as she left the room and went to get a blanket from the closet in the hall. The only satisfaction she derived from the situation was in knowing that he wasn't sleeping at Sharon Trappe's!

When Lee awoke the next morning, Jake was gone. The only sign of his ever having been there at all was the glass on the coffee table and the neatly folded blanket on one end of the sofa.

In the weeks that followed there were subtle changes in Lee's life that marked a new beginning. At first she struggled against the forces that seemed to be reshaping her life, but to no avail.

Her relationship, or rather her link, with Jake seemed weaker. Somehow, after the frightening experience in the desert and the brief stay in his apartment afterward, she'd broken loose from the emotional grip he'd held over her for so long. Upon first realizing this, Lee had felt naked, quite vulnerable. But closer inspection revealed that her close brush with death plus

Jake's ruthless methods of using her had shattered any illusions she might still have regarding him.

She'd heard it said that maturity, while a necessary ingredient for any well-adjusted person, was not always painless in its achievement. That was one timely saying she could certainly identify with. In her heart she'd berated herself time and again for her childish behavior as a wife, only to be forced to admit that Jake had contributed equally to the dissolution of their marriage.

Lee thought back to before they were married, how she'd refused to go to bed with him. In the end he'd offered marriage as a last resort, or so it seemed now. She also remembered the times when he'd almost driven her crazy with desire, his hands teasing her body until she became a writhing heap, her eyes dulled with passion. When he would finally take her, it seemed he did so with a calculating intentness. Other times his lovemaking took on the guise of unbelievable tenderness, satisfying her at every turn.

Lately she'd begun to wonder if Jake had unconsciously held her refusal to have an affair against her, if he'd thought she'd simply been angling for marriage to someone with his wealth and position.

Another decision she'd made was in her social life. No longer was she going to play it down, afraid to become involved. She'd firmly resolved that if she met someone interesting, she wouldn't withdraw. If it caused a confrontation with Jake, then so be it.

Although the stitches had been removed and her arm was back to normal, Lee's first day back at work was exhausting. The thought flitted through her mind that she might possibly be pushing herself, but idling away her time in her apartment was slowly driving her crazy. She knew she wasn't in any position to go out on a job, but she could certainly handle the paperwork, and the group she worked with were only too happy to oblige her.

"I used to envy you your cushy job or so I thought," remarked Diane Coler, an attractive redhead and a close friend. "But being shot . . . my God, Lee! That would have scared me to death."

"Believe me, I wasn't exactly a hero. Poor Simon. I'm afraid I gave him some bad moments," Lee confessed. They were having a leisurely lunch, catching up on all the office gossip.

"He needs some bad moments, and worse," Diane muttered as she took a sip of her drink. "I swear, he's getting more unbearable with every passing day. To put it bluntly, he's a pain in the buns!"

"Oh, my, such loyalty." Lee chuckled. "Is this the first peek at his other side?" she asked.

"Mmmm . . . yes and no. I've seen him tear into different people if he caught them shirking their responsibilities and justifiably so. But lately he seems to have turned all his disfavor my way. And you know me, Lee. I don't have this red mane for nothing." She sighed. "The worst thing is his sudden curiosity regarding my personal life."

"This gets more interesting by the second," Lee mused. "I still think your boss is jealous." At Diane's spluttered outburst of denial, Lee said, "I know all your reasons why he isn't, but how many bosses have you had who act as he does? And the two of you have gone out several times."

Diane shrugged, a rather pleased gleam showing in her eyes. "You don't think the trouble in Kuwait is behind his bad temper?"

"Oh, I'm sure he'll be glad when that little fiasco is resolved, but not to the extent you've described."

"Can Garrett Exploration absorb the loss if there has to be one?" Diane asked worriedly.

"I'm sure we can. Simon's too shrewd a businessman to risk everything on a venture in that region, especially knowing the temperament of the locals," Lee assured her.

Later on, when she found herself alone with him, Lee asked Simon much the same question that Diane had posed.

"Fortunately we're well covered. Otherwise it would have slowed us down temporarily." He gave her a speculative glance. "Are you worried that you'd find yourself out of a job?"

"Of course not," she quickly declared. "But I am concerned, and so are several others.

You're nice to work for . . . normally. Lately there's been a downward trend in your popularity," she informed him rather dryly.

"I see," he replied evenly. "Am I to assume this is your way of telling me to shape up?"

"A word to the wise is supposed to be sufficient," she added crisply. "You've an excellent staff who are used to working for a reasonably mild-mannered man. To suddenly find Attila the Hun at the helm has caused some speculation."

"Thank you, Mrs. Rhome, for your concern," he countered silkily. "Now I know why you were shot," he returned grimly. "I'm sure you were poking your nose in someone's business."

"Mmm," Lee murmured resignedly, dropping her gaze to the involved report she was working on. "I see what Diane was talking about."

"Ah, I might have known. That redheaded tyrant is at the bottom of this."

"Have you and Miss Coler had some sort of disagreement?" she asked innocently, her lips twitching suspiciously as she watched Simon.

"Disagreement hardly covers it. She's rude and bossy. She had the nerve to tell me that I was a pain in the . . ."

"Buns?" Lee quickly inserted before he could be more explicit.

"Precisely. She's an interfering witch."

"She's also very competent. Without her the engineers and geologists would resign. Through

91

some mysterious ability, she's able to decipher our scribblings, thereby enabling your operation to proceed without an unholy mixup. Without her you would suffer," Lee bluntly told him.

As the days wore on it became rather interesting to observe Diane and Simon in their own private battle. And unless Lee was completely off base, there appeared to be a relationship developing between them that was at times suspiciously akin to a romance.

Her relationship with Jake—or lack of one— seemed to be on hold, unless one cared to take into account the almost nightly telephone calls.

"I might have known you wouldn't do as I asked and stay home for a while longer," Jake drawled the second time he called. There was an acerbic quality in his voice that left Lee in little doubt of his disapproval.

"Don't be such a grouch, Jake," she chided him. "I'm merely doing some of the paperwork. It's very easy, very nonexhausting, and incredibly boring."

"And, of course, if you aren't sweating in some damned hot desert or risking life or limb in a civil war, you aren't happy, are you?"

"Did you call to start a fight, Jake?"

"Possibly," he answered tersely. "I wish to hell I knew."

Lee didn't question his remark, simply because there wasn't an answer.

It was a couple of days later and Lee was late leaving the office. She pulled the collar of her suede coat closer to keep out the sharp wind that cut through her like a knife. She hurried to the parking lot a half block away. By the time she reached her small compact car, her teeth were chattering.

She crosred her fingers as she inserted the key in the ignition, breathing a sigh of relief when it started on the first try. She'd been concerned about the battery for several days now and had planned on having a new one installed after work. Now it would have to wait until her lunch hour tomorrow, unless she could talk one of the men at the office into doing it for her.

The drive to her apartment was slower than usual, due to the light rain that began peppering down. Lee groaned wearily as she switched on the wipers. The inclement weather seemed to be the last straw. Hopefully her evening ahead with Mark, who had just returned from one of his business trips, would prove more enjoyable.

On reaching her apartment, she collected her mail and then unlocked the door. Once inside she scanned the letters on her way to the bedroom. Seeing that there was nothing of importance, she dropped them, along with her coat and handbag, onto a chair and began to undress. She eyed the tiny jeweled clock on her beside table and saw that she had exactly twenty-five minutes before Mark would arrive.

A short time later Lee stepped back from the full-length mirror, her hands smoothing the silken material of the light blue dress over her slim hips. It was a dress of simple design, also one that, to the discerning eye, bespoke an impressive price tag. With her tall, willowy figure Lee could wear the simplest garment and turn it into a stunning creation. Fortunately her salary allowed her to dress well, and as clothes were a weakness with her, most of her salary went for just that. And that, she chided herself, is why you never seem to have the money for a new car!

Lee quickly applied a light makeup base, eye shadow, and then blended a light blusher over her cheeks, accenting the almost classical lines of her face. After briskly brushing the curls that had replaced the long hair, she reached for the perfume bottle and touched the inside of each wrist. At that moment the doorbell rang. Lee picked up her small evening bag, fur wrap, and hurried out of the room.

The warmth of her greeting wasn't lost on Mark. While he wasn't foolish enough to make more out of it than it really was, it was nevertheless an added treat. He slid his arms around her in an easy embrace and gently touched his lips to hers. At her response the kiss turned into a lengthy one, leaving them both a bit breathless.

Mark drew back slightly, his hands clasped behind her waist, his blue eyes searching her face for an answer. Getting none, he said instead, "You're looking especially lovely this evening. Is there something I don't know about?"

"You're back. I'm looking forward to a lovely evening. What more could a girl ask for?" she responded in a teasing manner, an easy smile curving her inviting mouth.

"Mmm, that depends on the girl. But I'd be only too happy to suggest a couple of things," he answered in the same easy vein.

"Oh, I just bet you would." She laughed, moving out of his arms. She walked over to the sofa and reached for her bag and wrap. "Are you ready to go or would you like a drink first?"

"We'd better leave now. I made reservations for eight o'clock and it's pushing that now."

During the drive to the restaurant they talked, conversation coming easily. Since her return from her trip with Simon, this was the first time Lee had been out with Mark. She had told him all about her accident and her recovery and Mark's genuine relief and concern for her welfare deeply touched Lee. They had agreed from the beginning of their relationship to be friends and there were no rules about dating other people.

Mark's position on the legal staff of a large corporation based in Denver kept him busy. His schedule was subject to frequent trips to anywhere in the States and several foreign countries. This arrangement suited Lee. She knew it was these periods of absence that kept her interest alive in their friendship. At least that's what she kept telling herself. Closer scrutiny might have revealed an entirely different reason.

Much later, Lee leaned back in her chair, at the moment completely at peace with the world. The food had been everything Mark had promised and more. They'd started off with the smoked seafood appetizer with aquavit, and then on to saltimbocca, tender veal stuffed with cheese and prosciutto, followed by bittersweet chocolate mousse.

"More coffee, Lee?" Mark asked before dismissing the white-coated waiter.

"No, thank you," she murmured smilingly. "It's unfair to serve such food and then expect people to carry on as usual," she told him, the amount of wine she'd consumed accounting for the slight flush that heightened the slim contours of her face.

Mark smiled. "I agree," he said as he helped her with her wrap. With his hand at her elbow he guided her through the maze of snowy, linen-covered tables toward the exit. From there they went to a disco that was a favorite of theirs.

Upon entering the darkened establishment, Lee's foot was caught underneath one edge of a wide protective matting that covered a large expanse of the small entryway. At her slight stumble Mark's arm caught her, pulling her close to his side. She freed her foot of the restricting mat and turned her face up to his, laughing at her near accident.

"Can't you just see it now—me sprawling on

the floor in an ungainly heap? Immediately I'd be labeled as slightly drunk or worse."

"Actually I think you are—slightly drunk, that is." He laughed at her glare of mock rage, and then bent and kissed her. His action was so unexpected that Lee responded without thinking, the wine giving her a heady feeling.

"Excuse us, please," came an amused voice from close behind Mark. Immediately upon hearing those deep throbbing tones, Lee stiffened. What was Jake doing here?

"Darling, let's just squeeze by them. I'd hate to know we interrupted the course of true love," came the bored voice of his companion. "Although, if it were me, I'd prefer a more private place to indulge in a spot of lovemaking."

Mark, mistaking Lee's sudden withdrawal for embarrassment, threw a quick grin of apology over his shoulder, only to recognize Jake Rhome standing directly behind them. At that moment the situation became quite comical. For one brief moment Mark, before recognition registered in Jake's eyes, had a strong urge to take Lee by the arm and hurry her out of the disco. Before he could think further, Lee shifted position, her gaze clashing with that of her estranged husband's.

"Hello, Jake," Lee said, marveling that she could sound so carefree and at the same time control the tremor that was shooting through her body. "You know Mark." Her direct gaze moved to the attractive blonde, noting her possessive hold on Jake's arm.

Jake's curt greeting to Mark was brief, bordering on rude. He deliberately ignored Mark's outstretched hand, his icy stare blasting Lee with its intensity. In just seconds a blanket of tension was cast over the foursome that had Jake's date looking from him to Lee with more than a hint of question in her eyes.

At that moment the hostess appeared and informed Mark that their table was ready. He quickly grabbed Lee's arm and pushed her in the direction of the sequined back.

CHAPTER SIX

Once seated at their table Mark ordered drinks for them and then leaned forward and caught Lee's hand in his warm clasp. "Are you okay?" he asked, squeezing her fingers reassuringly. "You mustn't let him get to you this way, Lee." The forced gaiety and brittle smile on her lovely face left little doubt as to her true feelings at the moment.

"I'm fine, and he hasn't upset me, believe me. As a matter of fact, I find the whole thing amusing. The expression on Jake's face reminded me of a stern, disapproving parent."

That same look stayed with her throughout the evening. She knew it was there because she could feel it. She waged a silent battle, refusing to allow a resurgence of the old dominance he'd once held over her.

After Mark took her home, and she was in

bed, Lee congratulated herself on how well she'd handled Jake's presence at the disco. Although honesty demanded that she admit that it still hurt—these occasional encounters with him. But not to the extent they once had.

The next morning at her desk Lee regretted her eagerness of the night before to prove to Jake that she was enjoying herself. She'd never been one to imbibe too freely, always paying dearly the next day. And her latest foray was to be no exception, she grimly reflected.

She left her desk and went in search of Diane, who was finally run to ground in one of the consulting rooms. "Do you have any aspirin?" she asked without preamble, after waiting for another geogolist and an engineer to finish their business with the redhead.

"Sure," she replied. She eyed Lee critically as they made their way back to her desk. "Was it an evening of enjoyment or one of self-imposed punishment?" she asked knowingly.

Lee lifted one shoulder and gave her friend a rueful grin. "It started out rather nice, but we ran into Jake later, and that cast rather a disquieting pale over the festivities."

Diane laughed in spite of herself. "Did Mark stand his ground or did he allow Jake to intimidate him?"

"He did better than most of the others. The light of panic only surfaced briefly. Considering the unexpectedness of Jake, and his reputation, I think Mark handled it remarkably well." Lee loyally defended her friend.

"Mark is nice, but he's certainly not Jake," Diane muttered emphatically. By then they were at the office where Diane and another girl worked. She went over to her desk and rummaged in a drawer until she found the aspirin. "Keep them," she instructed Lee in a blunt voice. "I've a feeling you'll be needing them."

Lee, not known to be a shrinking violet, said, "Explain, please." She leaned against the edge of the desk and leveled a none-too-friendly look at her friend.

Diane sat down before answering. She leaned back in her chair, one hand absently playing with a pencil she held. "I know things are at cross purposes between you and Jake, Lee. I've been around since the beginning, remember? I also know him pretty well, and it's my opinion that he's taken about all he's going to from you."

"On what do you base this brilliant deduction?" Lee inquired coolly. Resentment flared at being placed in the position of having to defend her actions, especially to Diane. They'd been friends for years. Surely she wasn't going under the misguided belief that Jake was the injured party. True, the guilt was shared equally, but Lee felt she'd been hurt more than Jake.

"Common sense, Lee. And I'm surprised that you've let things build up to such an explosive state between the two of you."

That stung. Lee gave way to the anger that had been slowly building. "For your information, Miss Coler, Jake has half the women in

Denver thinking he's going to marry them. When he barged into my life in London, I thought, mistakenly so, that perhaps we did have a chance. By his actions and certain things he said it seemed perfectly reasonable to assume such. But I'd been in his apartment less than twenty-four hours when Sharon Trappe waltzed in like she was queen of the manor. Jake held up buying her engagement ring so that he could fly to London to get me. Last night he was with someone completely different." She paused in her blasting tirade. "I'm sorry, sweetie, but your analysis simply doesn't make sense. Jake might *desire* me, but that's all."

Diane arched her brows expressively and smiled. "A blind fool could see that he was almost out of his mind when he heard of the trouble you and Simon were in on that last trip. I've never seen anyone so upset."

"You saw Jake?" Lee asked, surprised.

"Yes. I was at lunch and ran into him. I casually mentioned that I was worried and explained why." Her expression sobered. "For a moment I thought he was going to pass out. From that minute until he left for London, I kept him informed of everything going on." She got up and walked around the desk to where Lee was standing. "Listen, honey, I know there are problems. I also know there's a great deal of pride involved. But don't settle for Mark Hayman just to prove a point."

A suspicious glimmer was visible in Lee's

blue eyes, brought on by what Diane had said. She lowered her gaze to the bottle she held in her hands, loathe to let anyone witness the feeling of regret that showed so plainly in her face. When she spoke, her voice was husky with emotion.

"I know you mean well and I appreciate it, really I do. But something happened, Diane, something I can't quite put my finger on. It's all tied up with that terrifying experience in the Middle East, and the time I spent in Jake's apartment. In the course of those few days I came to the conclusion that I had to get away from him completely." She shrugged her shoulders. "I'd begun to feel like a punching bag, and it wasn't very comfortable."

Their rather heated discussion stayed with Lee all through the day. One part of her desperately wanted to believe Diane's theory, but the seeds of distrust had been deeply planted and were not so easily discounted.

By the end of the day she wished they'd never even discussed Jake. An image of his stormy features taut with anger had haunted her all day. When she'd turned from Mark's kiss and encountered his burning gaze, it had been like receiving a blow to the midsection. For a moment they'd seemed alone in that crowded place. The noise of the music, the voices raised in conversation and laughter became mute in comparison. All she saw was his expression of anger and disgust—and for one brief second a look of utter defeat in his eyes. It had been shuttered so quickly Lee was almost doubtful of its existence.

On her way home from work Lee mentally ticked off the number of small chores that needed to be done. Since it was Friday, she debated giving the apartment a quick going-over and then leaving for the weekend. But where? With Mark away on one of his unexpected trips the two days stretched ahead like an eternity.

She thought of checking with Marta and Jim, and then decided against that idea. Those two were so in love they were hardly aware of anyone else. Perhaps Diane would want to get away. A weekend at a quiet ski lodge would be just the thing. Of course there'd be no snow as yet, she reasoned, but it would offer a change of pace that would be welcomed.

Once home, she changed from the tweed suit and cream-colored blouse to a pair of faded jeans and an old T-shirt that had seen better days. She set about stripping the bed and then gathered up the rest of her dirty clothes. Once those were in the washing machine, located in the small pantry-cum-laundry room off the kitchen, she put fresh sheets on the bed.

The kitchen was next on Lee's list. She was up to her elbows in sudsy water, cleaning the stove and the refrigerator, when the doorbell rang. A muttered "Damn" reflected her displeasure at the interruption. She grabbed a dishcloth and dried her hands as she padded to the door and opened it.

Jake was leaning against the door frame in a relaxed stance, casually clad in dark trousers, gray sweater, and a suede jacket with a sheepskin lining. His dark brows arched sharply at the sight of Lee's outfit. "Obviously you're dining in this evening," he stated in an amused voice as he pushed himself upright and entered the living room.

Lee experienced a flash of resentment as he brushed by her. "Do come in, Jake," she muttered sarcastically toward his broad back.

He merely threw her a wicked grin over one shoulder as he removed his jacket and dropped it onto a chair. "What's wrong, honey? Didn't your little interlude with Hayman last night come up to expectations?" he asked in a mocking voice.

"What are you doing here, Jake?" she demanded, remaining by the door, refusing to be drawn into a battle of words with him.

"Relax, Lee," he replied offhandedly. "It's seldom we get the chance to enjoy a quiet evening together. Let's make the most of it, shall we?"

Lee stared, incredulous. He made it sound as though they had difficulty arranging their schedules in order to spend an occasional evening together. Of all the nerve! She was further amazed when he sauntered over and switched on the stereo that was situated on the middle shelf of a bookcase built into a section of one wall of the room.

"Are you comfortable? Is there anything I

can get you?" she asked scathingly. Her chest heaved with outraged fury. The thin material of the T-shirt stretched taut across the thrusting fullness of her breasts. She wiped her sweaty palms on the dishcloth she still held, frantically searching her mind for some further insulting remark to hurl at Jake's menacing bulk.

"I'm quite comfortable, Lee," he said softly, turning from the stereo, the soft music lending a soothing background. "You can stop bristling like some kitten who's been scratched the wrong way, for I've no intention of leaving." There was a degree of roughness in his voice that Lee was very familiar with. If she forced the issue, she knew he would only retaliate in a way that would cause her to regret any rash action.

She glared icily at his stern countenance, but other than a resigned lift of her shoulders she refrained from commenting. "Enjoy yourself," she tossed flippantly over her shoulder as she stalked back to the kitchen.

Once there she attacked the cleaning with renewed vigor, anger at Jake giving her added energy. Damn him, when would he accept the fact that they were through?

"If you keep up this pace, you'll be exhausted," Jake growled from just behind her. One long arm reached over her shoulder and plucked the bottle of cleaner and the cloth from her hands. "Go take a shower, you've done enough," he instructed her in an authoritative voice.

"I find it difficult to believe you're so desperate for feminine companionship that you'd push your way in here, Jake," she blazed in an attempt to force his hand and rid herself of his disturbing company.

Heavy hands dropped to her shoulders and gripped them forcefully. "Desperation doesn't enter into it, Lee. If you're insinuating that sex is my only reason for being here, then you're wrong. That could be taken care of in less time than I think you care to admit," he growled, giving her a shake.

Lee raised tortured eyes to lock with his knowing ones, his words hurting her more than an actual blow. Her heart dictated that she give in to the traitorous feelings his close proximity was causing. But pride kept her from relenting, reminding her of the humilation she'd experienced the last time she'd weakened.

She reached up and grasped his strong wrists and removed them from her shoulders. "Please, don't let me stop you," she taunted. "Try the blonde you were with last night; she seemed eager enough." She turned on her heels and hurried from the room, not in the least reassured by the dangerous gleam that was visible in his dark eyes. When she reached her bedroom she slammed the door hard, feeling some measure of safety—regardless of how flimsy.

Lee stepped out of the jeans and walked into the bathroom to adjust the shower. She straightened and began to pull the T-shirt over her head when she felt the garment jerked from her hands and heard it rip as it was roughly dealt with and thrust aside. She turned on Jake, consumed with anger at his complete disregard for her privacy. "What in hell do you think you're doing?" she cried out furiously, grabbing at a towel and attempting to shield her body from his probing gaze.

"Taking what's rightfully mine," he said softly. Before she could twist by him, one arm slid neatly beneath her knees, another around her shoulders. She was lifted effortlessly and held against his broad chest.

"Put me down," she spluttered, pushing ineffectually at the hands still holding her captive.

"Gladly," he murmured determindedly, making his way into the bedroom and over to the bed.

Once there he dropped her in an ungainly heap. Lee stared up at him, her anger turning to perplexity. "What's gotten into you, Jake?" she whispered, tightly clutching the towel to her breasts. There was a determined glint in his eyes, the indomitable thrust of his jaw a clear indication of his mood.

He stood by the bed with his feet wide apart in a stance designed to stop her at the first sign of flight. His thumbs were caught in the waistband of his trousers, his entire posture one of authority. There was a controlled edge to his voice when he spoke. "I find it increasingly difficult to stand by and watch you flit from one man to another. I know what a passionate woman you are, Lee." His burning gaze lingered on the sheer brief bikini panties she wore and the knowing thrust of her breasts beneath the towel. "And I don't intend that anyone else enjoy that passion but me."

"Now, Jake, lis-listen to m-me," she stammered as she began to edge toward the other side of the bed, measuring the distance to the bathroom. It was a connecting bath between the two bedrooms, with a door that also opened onto the hall.

"Don't even think of it," he softly murmured, his ability to correctly interpret her thoughts shocking her.

"Leave me alone, Jake," she whispered, watching with sinking heart as he began to unbutton his shirt. "This won't solve anything between us—and you know it." She spoke hurriedly, her voice sounding high-pitched and nervous.

"Only time will tell," he replied mysteriously, one hand reaching out and switching off the lamp by the bed. Immediately the room was cast in almost total darkness with only the thin shaft of light from the partially opened bathroom door.

"Damn it, Jake, this has gone far enough," Lee cried, her voice sounding far braver than she actually felt. Keeping him at a distance was imperative. Being alone with Jake was the last thing she wanted, and especially in his present mood. There had never been a lack of passion in their lovemaking and he knew it. But to allow him to take advantage of that fact was repugnant.

The darkened room prevented Lee from seeing his face, but the deep-throated chuckle that escaped him caused goosebumps to rush to the surface of her skin. The light rustle of clothing being discarded was the only other sound. She quickly secured the towel more snugly about her body and then slid one leg over the edge of the bed. Her foot eased to the floor, her muscles becoming taut in anticipation of her escape.

Suddenly Jake lunged across the bed, blindly reaching out for Lee. One hand grasped a naked thigh, while the other caught a substantial portion of the towel, flinging it aside. She twisted her body in hopes of breaking his hold, but Jake grabbed a handful of hair instead.

Lee's sharp cry of pain was mingled with the heavy breathing and the scuffle that ensued between them. "You're hurting me," she ground out between clenched teeth, her fists pounding against the solid wall of his chest as he hauled her back across the bed, using his legs to control her wild kicking.

"Then stop fighting me," Jake muttered. He let his full weight fall on her, effectively bringing an end to her struggles. He caught both her hands and held them pinned to the bed above her head. The other hand moved to cup her . "I didn't mean this to happen, but it's n to the point that I can't control my feel- actions where you're concerned." He rshly.

"The great Jake Rhome not in control of his every thought? I find that difficult to believe. What you're really mad about is seeing me enjoying myself with another man, isn't it, Jake?" she snarled. "You can't bear to think that Mark has made me happy—and he has, believe me," she taunted dangerously, completely disregarding the bone-crushing grip on her wrist. Had she been able to see his face, she would have been shocked at the look of utter desolation that flitted across his rough features before being replaced by a murderous look of rage.

"Then I hope those memories will last forever, because I intend seeing Mark Hayman destroyed," he growled savagely, his mouth swooping down on hers in a brutal attack.

Suddenly a fire began in the sensitive tips of Lee's breasts that were crushed against the hair-rough chest. Her lips were forced apart and Jake's tongue invaded the soft sweetness of her mouth. Slowly her resistance began to fade as the burning flames of desire licked at her.

It wasn't until her arms stole around his neck, her fingers threading themselves through the raven-black thickness of his hair, that Lee realized he'd released his hold. His hands were taken up with teasing her body to that pitch one experiences just prior to leaping from a precipice. The fingers of one hand slowly worked their way down her back, lingering on each familiar spot of arousal, while his other hand was involved in an erotic assault on her breasts.

Lee gave up all thought of fighting him as she

joined him in the bittersweet game of assuaging their desire for each other. When Jake muttered protestingly at the thin strip of lace that offered only a slight barrier against his probing caresses, Lee unconsciously lifted her hips, enabling him to strip the panties from her body.

As his hand moved along her thighs in a teasing motion of touching and stroking, Lee arched her hips convulsively, a low moan escaping from her.

"Does Mark make you feel this way, Lee?" Jake whispered mockingly. His mouth moved down and caught one nipple between his lips, giving it a sharp tug. "Does he do this? Or this?" he whispered, his hand never ceasing its arousing manipulations.

The mocking words brought home the realization of her weakness where Jake was concerned. It swept over her like a rush of cold air. It wasn't part of her future plans to meekly submit to the dictates of Jake. She withdrew her hands from his shoulders and pushed against his chest.

Jake raised his head and stared at her in the darkness. "What's wrong, honey, did the mention of your lover cause the guilt to stop you?" he asked roughly.

"And if it did?"

"I'm afraid you'll have to learn to live with it, for I've no intention of stopping—now or ever."

"Don't you ever grow weary of riding rough-

112

shod over people?" Lee asked, knowing even as she asked the ridiculous question that he'd won.

"Never. At least not when it affords me such pleasure as this," he answered, his mouth lowering to hers. Their lips clung together, hungry for the taste of each other. They were forged together in a burning anguish, bordering on desperation. The bronze hue of his skin hovered only a second over the whiteness of hers before they came together, their breathing reduced to gasps of unbelievable joy and groans of pleasure.

Twice more during the night Lee was awakened by the demanding caresses of Jake's hands on her body. One part of her shrieked out against the bold intrusion of this man in her life, but her senses ignored the warning. It was as though she were caught up in a maelstorm of emotion and desire, consumed with a deeper need for Jake than anything else in the world.

CHAPTER SEVEN

Lee surfaced slowly through the clouds of sleepiness, pushing at the annoying "thing" that was tickling her nose. Her hand was caught and held against something warm and slightly scratchy. Large blue eyes opened in surprise only to be met and held by warm teasing brown ones.

"Good morning, sleepyhead," Jake murmured huskily, moving her hand from his cheek to press his lips against her palm.

Lee felt a telltale flush spread over her face as his knowing gaze moved over her, lingering on one rose-tipped breast touching his chest. She was even further disconcerted to discover her leg casually thrown over Jake's in complete abandonment.

When she would have drawn the sheet up to her shoulders and removed her leg, he stopped her on both moves. "Don't cover yourself from me," he gently whispered. "I enjoy seeing your body and feeling it against mine."

"Please, Jake," she protested, her gaze dropping under the burning intentness of his. "You're embarrassing me."

"Why, Lee?" he demanded on a harsher note. "This isn't the first time I've seen you without clothes and, I promise you, it won't be the last. You're my wife; you belong to me." One large hand reached out and gently cupped her breast in a clearly possessive gesture.

"You seem to be forgetting that we're separated, Jake, and I don't belong to anyone," she pointed out teasingly. She knew she was playing a dangerous game, but for the moment she refused to listen to the warnings being flashed in her mind. She was fully alive for the first time in weeks. Surely the gods would allow her these few hours.

"You don't honestly think I'll sit idly by and allow you to drift from one meaningless affair to another, do you?"

"Frankly the thought hasn't occurred to me. But on the other hand, I really can't see why it should concern you."

Jake chuckled, amusement rather than the anger she'd expected crowding his dark eyes. "I'd be careful if I were you, honey. Teasing has a way of backfiring."

Later, as she showered, Lee recalled that moment and the unmistakable warning behind the facade of humor. Then there was the threat he'd

115

uttered against Mark. Albeit in the throes of possessive anger, it bothered her.

She turned off the shower and reached for a fluffy towel. After drying herself she hurried to the bedroom and put on fresh panties and bra. She then added a pair of cream wool slacks and a cable-stitch sweater of the same color. Several quick strokes of the brush took care of her hair. Lip gloss and a light touch of eye shadow completed her toilet.

As soon as she opened the bedroom door her nose was assailed with the tantalizing aroma of bacon frying. *He's making himself quite at home,* she thought with a rueful twist of her mouth, *and I've never felt less like a fight.*

Lee took a deep breath, hoping to dispel the strange, light-headed sensation that was gripping her. Involvement with Jake was promising to be an exhausting experience.

When she entered the kitchen Jake looked up from where he was carefully stirring scrambled eggs. His sharp gaze took in the faint smudge beneath her eyes and the paleness of her face.

"I hope you have a huge appetite this morning. All I want is some toast," she said by way of greeting.

"Nonsense. From the looks of you, you've been skipping too many meals lately." He reached for a mug and poured a cup of coffee. "Here, take this and sit down. I'll join you in just a few minutes."

Lee took the coffee and did as he instructed. A brief smile tugged at one corner of her mouth as she watched him move about her small kitchen. Her eyes were drawn to his dark hair, still damp from his shower. She could smell his clean male scent from where she sat at the table. Even her cat had gone over to the enemy. Tom, as with most cats, was quick to see where the most chicken livers were to be had. From the amount in his bowl, it was evident Jake had given him two days' portion in one.

It was a familiar scene, with Jake doing the cooking while she sipped coffee. Lee had never bothered with breakfast before marrying him. This had amazed Jake. So on the weekends he'd always taken over the preparation of the meal himself. Since they'd parted, Lee had fallen back into her old routine of a cup of coffee, a glass of juice, or, most times, nothing. Obviously from the set of his jaw, Jake didn't approve. But then, that was no surprise; he hadn't approved of anything she'd done in quite a while, Lee reminded herself.

So intent was her examination of Jake and the past that she jumped when his arm brushed hers as he set a plate before her loaded with generous portions of eggs, bacon, and two slices of toast!

"Have I suddenly sprouted horns?" he asked with scarcely a break in his movements as he served himself.

"N-no," she stammered, mentally cursing herself for her lapse. Remembering the more pleasants moments of their marriage was a foolish indulgence. And if Jake ever knew of such

117

a weakness, he'd be sure to use it against her. *No, my dear,* she chided herself reprovingly, *this is not the time for gentle reminiscing. Rather, you should be trying to find some way to stop these encounters with Jake.*

"Aren't the eggs done to your liking?" he casually asked as he took his seat opposite her.

"They're fine, but I'm not hungry. As a matter of fact, nothing has tasted really good for several days now. Half the people in our office have been out with a virus. I suppose I'll be next."

"Mmm, perhaps you should see your doctor. That accident probably took more out of you than you're admitting," he replied smoothly.

For a moment Lee thought she must be hearing things. The Jake she knew or thought she knew would normally have raised the roof at her not eating. Now here he was calmly accepting her explanation without any show of temper. She eyed him suspiciously over the rim of her glass while she sipped the orange juice he'd thoughtfully set by her plate.

He raised his dark eyes and met her gaze boldly, perfectly aware of the puzzlement growing inside her. His next question caught her completely off guard. "Do you have plans for the weekend?"

"No."

"Good. I thought I'd ride up to the cabin and check it out before winter really sets in. How about coming with me?"

The idea was very appealing. She was also

pleased that he hadn't sold the property, and told him so.

"Why would I want to sell it?"

"Well," she shrugged. "We did spend our honeymoon there."

His enigmatic gaze held hers, leaving her baffled by its intensity. "There's a great deal you don't know about me, Lee. It seems incredible that you could have stayed married to me for two years and still be so ignorant of my ways. As for the cabin," he told her with a straight face, "the property surrounding it makes it an excellent investment."

"I see," she sharply answered, her fingers tearing a piece of toast into tiny bits. She missed the flash of amusement that flitted across his tanned face.

"I doubt that you do, but we'll leave it for now. Can you be ready in an hour?"

"I'm not sure—"

"Lee," he spoke in a resigned voice. "Don't be such a coward. You want to go just as much as I want you to. For once admit it and stop this damn quibbling."

His open criticism was too much. "Is that how you see it, Jake? Mere quibbling?" she asked, her voice trembling with emotion, tears blurring her vision.

"Quibbling, fighting, arguing . . . what's the difference? It all boils down to the same thing. Me, prodding, demanding, with you digging in your heels like a stubborn little mule."

Lee found herself at a loss for words, her

outburst momentarily forgotten. For Jake was right, their relationship, including their marriage, had been an unholy struggle between two very strong-willed individuals.

"Unfortunately I'm forced to agree with you," she murmured. "That's the reason I've finally come to a decision regarding a divorce. I honestly think we'd both be a lot happier if we knew our marriage was over . . . ended. The way we are now, this frustrating limbo, is as nerve-racking as our marriage was."

"And you think a divorce would solve our problems?" Jake asked harshly. He was leaning back in his chair, his thumbs hooked in the waistband of his trousers, his dark gaze riveted on Lee's face. "Would it stop the love we have for each other? Can a piece of paper cut through emotions, feelings, the deep concern that two people have for each other?"

Lee found herself unable to face the questions or Jake's compelling gaze. She looked down at her plate. For the first time, she felt the faintest quiver of guilt—or was it regret—at the bold stand she'd made regarding her career. It wasn't a comfortable feeling, nor did she allow herself to dwell on it. After all, she'd worked and slaved to get where she was. If anything, there should be pride in that accomplishment.

"May I ask you a question, Lee?" Jake broke into her thoughts. She raised her head and looked at him, wondering, as she did, how it was possible for two intelligent adults to make such a muddle of their lives.

"Certainly."

"What would you say to a sort of truce? Perhaps even a last-ditch effort to save our marriage?"

Lee sat stunned, not believing her ears. After all they'd done to each other, the deep scars they'd left, was he actually proposing that they have another go at destroying each other?

"You're either very brave or totally insensitive. We know what our problems are. I can't accept the role you demand I play, and you can't accept my career." She leaned forward, a curious sadness in her voice when she spoke. "Why prolong it, Jake?"

He was silent for an electrified moment and then said, "Because I can't and won't accept that we've failed." He sat forward, reaching out and catching her slim hand in his warm grasp. "Come to the cabin with me for the weekend. At least give yourself time to think about what I've said." He shook his dark head in a gesture of weariness. "I'm well aware that you have doubts, fears. So do I. But, honey, we still have an awful lot of love going for us. And in my book that counts for something."

"What about after the weekend?" Lee quietly asked, refusing even to think of his plan succeeding.

"That has to happen at will. We won't force it. I will say this though. I promise not to harass you about your job, even though your last assignment was a little extreme."

In her heart Lee felt the same. To her dismay,

she also realized that going back to Kuwait wasn't nearly as appealing as it had been.

"What do I have to do if I accept this trial period you're suggesting?"

Jake gave her a thoughtful look. "I don't think we need a lot of rules, do you? Who knows, if you go with me to the cabin, you might not even want to take it further."

"But surely, if this . . . this idea is to work, we both have to compromise," she pointed out in an unexpected defense of his suggestion.

The glimmer of hope that surfaced in the brown depths of Jake's eyes was quickly masked. "True. But I'd say more from my point of view than yours. I have to get used to the idea of my wife preferring to read core samples than cookbooks. I think I can accept that now."

Somehow this bit of news failed to lend the excitement that Lee had always imagined his acceptance of her career would give her, which was ridiculous, considering she'd spent almost three years of her life fighting him for just such an admission.

Later, seated beside Jake in the luxurious comfort of the dark Lincoln he drove, Lee had time to ponder the wisdom of accepting the wild proposal put to her.

There was one particular thing that had surprised her even more than the idea itself, that being Jake's voluntary agreement to accept her career and the erratic schedule she kept. All in all the last twelve hours had been most eventful!

She sneaked a peek at Jake, seeing the implacable outline of his profile, the same indomitable thrust of chin and jaw. There was no outward difference that she could see, so what had happened to cause him to make such a complete turnaround? This perplexing thought stayed with Lee during most of the trip, nagging her with its conflicting image of the man she thought she knew so well, and obviously didn't.

"If this weather holds, I might be able to catch some nice trout for our dinner." Jake broke the companionable silence. "Care to join me?" he asked, throwing Lee a purely mischievous grin, knowing full well her dislike for the sport.

Not to be outdone, Lee lifted her chin a fraction, giving him her coolest smile. "I'd be delighted."

Jake raised one dark brow at this sweeping statement, his lips twitching at the thought of her reaction if she really did catch a fish. "What made you change your mind?" he asked curiously.

"I'm not sure," she confessed. "But for you to spend so much time at it, it must have hidden pleasures. At least," she added saucily, "that way I can keep you honest. I won't have to listen to any more wild tales about the huge one that got away."

"I see. You're really not enamored of the idea, but you'll endure so that I'll keep my stories straight?"

"Something like that." She grinned, realizing how easy it was to fall in with the easy banter.

She was with her husband, and she was enjoying herself.

Jake didn't comment, but from his relaxed air, Lee knew she'd pleased him. Though how she was going to get through such a boring activity as fishing, she wasn't sure.

When they rounded the sharp curve in the highway and turned onto the narrow road that would take them past two other cabins and eventually to Jake's, Lee's excitement grew. For whether or not she cared to admit it, the happiest moments of her marriage, of her life, had taken place along the narrow road in the woods surrounding the cabin and in the cabin itself. Naturally loving the outdoors, she'd spent hours walking, picking wildflowers, even taking naps beneath the blue sky.

Looking back, she knew it was the only time she and Jake had been totally free of conflict in their relationship, which deteriorated continually until that final week when the subject of babies and her giving up her job had shattered it completely.

Jake, noting the pensive silence she'd lapsed into and the thoughtful expression on her face, asked, "Painful memories?"

"Oh, no," Lee quickly replied, turning her head and smiling at him. "Actually it was the other way around. Our honeymoon was the happiest time of my life." Her voice grew husky with the admission.

"Then perhaps it was intended that we start

124

this new beginning here. At least we both have pleasant thoughts about the place."

Lee refrained from commenting, for at that moment they were right at the cabin and the sight of the fieldstone-and-timber structure was like a beckoning refuge reaching out to her.

It was impossible for her to mask the excitement she felt at the moment. She turned a beaming face to Jake, who had switched off the engine and was watching her. "It's just as I remembered," she said softly. "Thank you for asking me." Without stopping to think, she slid across the seat and kissed him on the cheek. When she would have drawn back, Jake stopped her, his arms sliding easily around her and holding her close.

"I know I said I was willing to change my thinking on some things, honey, but making love to you isn't one of them." His mouth covered hers in a kiss that soon had Lee responding with a fervor that matched his own.

It was Jake who finally pulled back, his breathing ragged, as though he'd been running for miles. He eased back from Lee, enough so that he could look down into her face. "Why?" he murmured in a rasping voice. "Why in God's name do I have this unbelievable weakness where you're concerned?" He let his hands slip upward to frame her face, one thumb gently caressing her bottom lip. "Do you use some kind of secret potion on me, Lee?" he softly asked, his brown gaze burning with intensity.

Lee remained motionless beneath his touch.

The same smoldering desire that held Jake's features taut had left her defenseless. There was a mute appeal for understanding in her eyes, a vulnerability that caused him to slowly draw her to him, his chin resting against her hair.

"It's got to work, honey. Some way, somehow, it's up to us to find it."

This time when he set her back from him he was more in control, even to the point of smiling. "Shall we go in?" he murmured.

Lee could only nod her head. A sixth sense warned her that they'd passed some sort of milestone in their stormy relationship. There had been no blinding light or thundering voice declaring such an event taking place; merely an intuitive flash in the back of her mind.

Jake unlocked the front door and stepped aside to allow Lee to enter the familiar den. She let her eyes follow a circuitous route of the room, unprepared for the tears that blurred her vision or the lump that rose in her throat as she stood silently, letting the familiar surroundings soothe her battered spirits.

A slight noise behind her reminded Lee that Jake was waiting with their luggage. She managed to blink back the tears before turning to face him. "I'll start opening the windows while you bring in the groceries." As she started to move away, he stopped her, catching her upper arm in a light hold.

"Lee? Are you sure you want to stay?" he asked, concern evident in his stance and his voice.

She smiled. "Of course, I'm sure." Suddenly there was a devilish glint in her blue eyes. "Are you trying to weasel out of our fishing expedition?"

"Oh, no," he growled. "I don't regret a single thing I've said this day."

Lee knew the implication went much further than mere fishing. It also put her at a disadvantage, or did it? Her dealings with Jake had always been with her on the defensive, and him as the aggressor. Now it seemed that Jake was subjecting her to a gentle, determined wooing, and whether or not it was all in vain, she liked it.

There was an easy, relaxed mood as they went about the task of airing out the cabin. Lee put away the groceries and made decisions regarding lunch and dinner in case no trout were available, while Jake checked the supply of firewood, the storm windows, and various other things on his list.

Lee had just turned from the refrigerator, her hands clutching a head of lettuce, some sliced ham, and a jar of mayonnaise, when Jake opened the back door and entered the kitchen.

There was open pleasure in his face at the sight of Lee in the kitchen, and he did nothing to mask it. "Is that coffee I smell?" he asked, going over to the sink and washing his hands.

"Yes, but only if you stop washing up in my kitchen," Lee answered sternly, eyeing the sudsy water on the lip of the sink and the surrounding counter.

"Yes, ma'am," Jake intoned solemnly, reaching for a wad of paper towels and quickly cleaning up the mess he'd made. He turned to Lee, an engaging grin on his face. "Am I forgiven?"

Lee considered him dubiously. "I suppose so. How many sandwiches can you eat?"

"Three or four." He spoke over his shoulder as he got down two mugs and filled them with coffee.

"You'll get fat," she told him frowningly. "Besides, that much bread isn't good for you."

"Do you think I've put on weight?" he asked quietly, leaning his considerable frame against the counter where she was working.

"Vanity, Jake?" Lee teased. "Maybe just the tiniest roll about your waist," she continued to tease. He was in excellent physical condition, and he knew it.

"I see," he mused. "I thought it was something else you were concerned with, like me making love to you, while all you were doing was determining if I was putting on weight. Tsk, tsk. I must be losing my touch."

"Oh, you idiot." Lee laughed. "There's not an ounce of difference in your weight and you know it. And," she spoke daringly, at the same time shoving the plate of sandwiches in his hands, "I really wasn't interested in your measurements at the time." Her blue eyes turned dark with remembered passion.

CHAPTER EIGHT

The small creek that meandered through the edge of Jake's property was fed by a much larger river to the north. Lee sat on the creek bank, her back comfortably resting against the trunk of a scrub oak.

Her gaze touched lightly on the water in its ever-moving flow, on to where Jake was casting, standing mid-thigh in the water a bit up the creek, and back to the red cork he had attached to her own fishing line.

She still wasn't sure what had caused her to agree to this insane idea, but she had and it was promising to be quite restful. Certainly not as wildly exhilarating as Jake made it out to be, nevertheless it was pleasant enough.

Her eyes felt heavy. Lunch and the soothing effects of the outdoors made her drowsy. Lee yawned hugely and gave in to the gentle pull of sleep that tugged at her, letting her head relax against the tree, her eyes closing.

Suddenly the rod and reel she held in her lax hands gave a jerk. Almost at the same time she heard Jake yell, "Watch your cork!"

Lee came to her feet with a startled leap, her mind frantically trying to recall all the things Jake had told her to do. Set the hook first, he'd instructed, or had he? Reel steadily, keeping the line taut. But he'd failed to point out that a person was likely to forget which came first and would, in all probability, freeze, which is exactly what Lee did.

"Jake," she yelled excitedly, "I've got one! I've got one," scrambling about and tugging for dear life as she sought to bring in her catch by moving in a backward direction.

"Use your reel, honey," Jake instructed laughingly as he made his way out of the water toward her.

"I can't remember how the damn thing works," she yelled breathlessly just as one foot became entangled in a small clump of weeds and vines. The next minute Lee was flat on her back, a determined look on her face, a death grip on the rod.

By the time Jake reached her, she was struggling to her knees. "Don't let me lose it, Jake. I'm sure it must be huge," she recklessly boasted, oblivious to the dust and dirt on her face and clothes.

"Oh, at least . . ." Jake blandly agreed, effectively masking his amusement. He lifted her to her feet and at the same time managed to guide her hands to the proper placements, helping her to reel in the trout.

In her excitement it seemed that Lee still preferred to pull her fish from the water, necessitating Jake to stand behind her in order not to have a fishing line stretched the one hundred yards or so from cabin to creek!

"I believe you'll find it simpler, Lee, to use the reel," he spoke in a voice trembling with suppressed laughter.

"Don't you dare laugh at me, Jake Rhome!" she exclaimed.

When the chore was completed and Jake held the trout up for Lee's inspection, she was positively bubbling over with excitement.

"I can't believe it," she kept repeating, "I simply can't believe it." Suddenly there appeared a thoughtful, guarded gleam in her eyes as she left her admiration of her fish and looked at Jake. "How long is it?" she demanded.

"Er, you mean how much does it weigh, don't you?" he grinned.

"Whatever." She waved one hand dismissively. "Is it as big as the ones you've caught today?" She challenged him on a high of excitement that was unexplainable.

"Well," Jake said slowly, "I believe yours fits nicely in the middle. I've caught one larger and one smaller."

Lee turned her head and looked at the

lengthening shadows, her lips pursed determinedly. "There's still time to do some more fishing, isn't there?"

"Of course. As a matter of fact, since you're so enthusiastic, I'll call it a day and sit here with you. It might save me a doctor bill," he tacked on innocently.

"Never mind," Lee answered, sending him a blazing glare. "I want to catch the biggest fish."

It occurred to Lee later, as she stood beneath the shower and let the warm water cleanse her body of the accumulated dirt from her outing, that the day had been one of the nicest she'd spent in a long time. The fishing had been an added bonus. She hadn't thought once of her job, of where she'd be sent next. It had been enough that she was with Jake—a Jake who seemed totally different somehow.

But what about after the weekend? Lee asked herself. Would there still be the same understanding, the same easy acceptance? Probably not. It would be almost humanly impossible for a man as strong as Jake to suddenly accept her career, especially when it had been one of the main issues in the dissolution of their marriage.

Don't analyze the situation to death, a tiny voice whispered. *You're with Jake and there's hope, albeit faint, for your marriage. Give it a chance.*

Lee sighed as she turned off the water and reached for a towel. If she didn't put a stop to such negative thoughts, she'd panic and run. But there was so much at stake, also scars not yet healed. Dare she risk the rapier-sharp edge of Jake's anger when she would be forced to be away for days, even weeks, with him swallowing his displeasure until he exploded?

There was a pensive look about her as she emerged from the bathroom and entered the master bedroom. Jake hadn't asked if she would share his bed, merely assumed so. Lee hadn't protested. Why bother? She *wanted* to sleep with her husband, *wanted* to feel his arms around her the last thing at night and the first thing each morning.

God, she thought remorsefully, flinging aside the towel and walking over to the closet, *but your thinking is screwed up. First you're suspicious of Jake's every move. On the other hand, you want every minute, every second with him, dreading the end of these idyllic two days.*

During the short time it took her to dress in a light-blue caftan, brush her hair into a shining riot of curls, and join Jake in the kitchen, Lee had managed to submerge the doubts and fears that had tarnished the precious moments she'd spent with Jake.

"Feeling better?" he asked as she joined him at the counter and began putting together a salad from the freshly washed vegetables waiting in the large aluminum colander in the sink.

"Definitely." She smiled at him. "It would have been nice to take a long soak, but I wasn't sure if you'd give my catch the proper care." She grinned engagingly, still feeling an enormous pride in her ability the first time out.

"Oh, I did, I assure you. No fish has ever been so delicately handled. I'm sure it will melt in your mouth. By the way," Jake remarked, forking the last of the trout from the frying pan and placing it on the platter, "you look particularly beautiful tonight. Did you remember that I like you in blue?"

Lee kept her eyes on the tomato she was slicing, suddenly shy of this man she loved. She felt rather than saw Jake move up behind her. When his arms snaked out and clasped her around the waist and drew her back against him, Lee relaxed, letting her body absorb the warmth and feel of him. How could something that was so right, so good, between two people turn into a nightmare of despair?

"What's wrong, Lee?" Jake murmured against her ear, his hands slowly caressing the curve of her hips, inching upward over waist and midriff to cup her breasts.

"Wrong?" she echoed.

"Yes. You're trying very hard to be bright and cheerful. But your body is tense and there's a forced gaiety in your voice. You've changed since we came in from fishing. Was it something I said?"

"No, it's nothing you've done, Jake. It's just—"

"Memories?" he asked roughly. He spun her around to face him. "Don't let past mistakes cloud your reasoning, Lee. All right, so we had a rough two years. To be blunt, most of it was pure hell. But there were moments . . . a brief

134

glimpse into a relationship that could have been wonderful. As today was, even last night," he growled.

"But that's just it, Jake. Last night . . . today. Are we fooling ourselves? Is it too late?" There was a huskiness to her voice, a look in her eyes of pleading.

"No," Jake answered harshly. "If we love each other enough, we can make it work. If the love's not there, then"—he shrugged his broad shoulders—"nothing we do can save it."

"I do love you, Jake," Lee whispered, her blue eyes locking with his dark ones.

"I know, sweetheart, I know." His hands went to the tensed muscles of her neck and shoulders, his fingers gently kneading the tautness there. "We have the love. Now we have to find a way to live together." He considered her thoughtfully and said, "I'm willing to try. Are you?"

Lee gave him a ghost of a smile. "Do you mean am I willing to have another go at being a housewife?" She dropped her gaze to the tanned column of his throat, unconsciously chewing at her bottom lip. "I need time, Jake. I want you and my career." She spoke honestly. "Does that make me sound hard and unyielding?"

"A little." He grinned. "But no more so than I am. We're both faced with priorities—what's most important."

There was a short pause as Lee struggled with the commitment facing her. Did she even want to become embroiled again in the complicated task of juggling a career and a marriage? Of trying to keep Jake happy, and at the same time taking advantage of the opportunities that came her way? "What if I fall flat on my face from the effort?"

"Then I suppose I'll just have to pick you up again," he countered smoothly. "Anything else?"

"Oh, yes. But at the risk of sounding redundant I'll let it pass."

"Good. Let's eat. Reconciliations have a way of making me hungry," said Jake. Before Lee could move from the circle of his arms, he bent his head and touched his lips to hers. It wasn't a kiss meant to point out the obvious passion that could blaze between them at a mere touch, a look, but simply a gesture of love, of understanding.

After dinner the cleaning up was shared. Lee protested that since he'd done the cooking she should do the dishes. But Jake was adamant. It occurred to her that perhaps he too was dreading the time when they would be apart, that he wanted to share each moment they had.

When the kitchen was back to its original order, Jake took two glasses from the cupboard and a bottle of wine from the refrigerator. There was a fire going in the fireplace in the den, and Lee soon found herself settled on the sofa with Jake's head in her lap.

There was music in the background from the cassette Jake had flipped in place, the sound soothing and unobtrusive. Lee stared at the leaping flames in the fireplace, refusing to allow bad thoughts to infringe on the moment. It was perfect—a warm fire to take the chill off the autumn evening, good wine, soft music, and Jake in her arms. An unconscious sigh of contentment escaped her, bringing Jake's intense gaze to rest on her face.

"Happy?" he murmured, catching her hand that was lying on his chest and pressing the palm to his lips.

"Can't you tell?" Lee smiled down at him. Her free hand buried itself in the raven thickness of his hair, her thumb gently caressing the thick sideburns and the chiseled granite of his cheek, glorying in the feel, the nearness of him.

"Show me," he commanded in the throbbing tones of a lover, his tongue tracing a sensitive pattern on her palm and the wildly beating pulse in her wrist.

"No," she answered provocatively, watching him through the thick, gold-tipped lashes that fringed her eyes. In a gesture that was bold and daring, she let the tip of her pink tongue slowly moisten her lips, some inner demon egging her on, urging her to assume the role of enchantress.

Jake's eyes darkened perceptibly at this open invitation on her part, his v̶
flashing in contrast to his tanned
smiled at the challenge he saw in h̶
you sure, Lee? No more regret
huskily.

"None that I can't handle," she whispered daringly. Before the words were out of her mouth, she found herself flat on her back with Jake's body covering hers, pressing her farther into the cushions.

He levered himself up on one elbow and stared down at her. "I should have known." He brought his hand up and cradled her face. "You pretend to dislike the demanding side of me when it's your career we're discussing; but when it comes to making love you scream out for dominance. Why is that? I wonder."

Lee didn't have an answer. Humiliating though it was, she knew he spoke the truth. Perhaps it was the realization that in bed he brooked no argument. He could even take her anger at him and turn it into a blazing torrent of desire, gnawing at her, nipping at her, until, helpless against his onslaught, she returned pleasure for pleasure, sated and whole.

"Does it matter?" she murmured, giving an indrawn gasp of pleasure as one hand left her face and slipped inside the plunging neckline of the caftan and cupped a breast.

"Not in the least, honey," he said matter-of-factly, pushing at the shimmery material until one shoulder and creamy mound were bare. His head bent and his mouth took over where his hand had so excited her. Lee turned her head from side to side in a restless, unfulfilled moment, wanting to feel his touch on all of her body and impatient for what she knew was coming.

138

As though perfectly attuned to her thoughts and the needs of her body, Jake pushed himself into a sitting position on the edge of the sofa. He reached down and caught the hem of the caftan and pulled it up over Lee's hips, shoulders, and lastly her head, dropping it in a heap on the floor. Next came the lacy briefs, and they too joined the blue garment on the floor.

Lee watched, entranced, as Jake stood and began to remove his own clothing, her gaze skimming greedily over the wide shoulders and hair-rough chest, the powerful torso tapering to a trim waist. When the last vestige of covering was gone, they moved toward each other, two separate parts, but of one being, controlled by a single entity.

When Lee would have hurried the final moment, Jake slowed it. His hands and mouth became masters of exquisite torture as they sought the gentle curves of her hips, the delicate sloping of her slim, white thighs, and paid homage to the thrusting proudness of her breasts, the rose tips straining out for their own share of erotic titillation.

Amid this onslaught of desire drawing Lee farther and farther into its swirling center, she found herself wanting to mete out the same sort of enjoyment to Jake, wanted him to share in the dizzying heights of ecstasy now flooding her entire being.

Her fingers became as light as the delicate fluttering of butterfly wings in their own deter-

mined course of seduction. Her lips tantalized
in their quest of the taste and smell of him as
she kissed his nipples, the hollow in his neck,
and finally his lips. Jake luxuriated in the
warmth of their heated arousal, reminding Lee
of a large, sleek tom cat, his own gasps of pleasure like the deep purring of his feline counter-
part.

Suddenly the limits of restraint were reached.
Jake settled fully on top of her soft, quivering
body, his thighs sliding against Lee's. His entrance into that most sensitive part of her was
quick and strong, driving her into a frenzy of
excitement.

Lee clung to Jake with every fiber of her
being, her only thought the spiraling sensation
that intensified with each dizzying thrust. And
then the entire world exploded, tossing them
mercilessly upward on a course devoid of all
sight, sound, and awareness, culminating in a
state of unbelievable calm and peace.

It was a long while later when Lee became
aware of being lifted and held in a warm embrace. "Jake?" she murmured drowsily.

"Shh . . . I'm taking you to bed," the deep
voice sounded against her hair.

She slid her arms around his neck and snuggled against the crisp roughness of hair on his
chest. "Are you coming to bed now?"

"Oh, yes," Jake murmured. "The appetizer
was most tasty. I can't wait for the main
course."

Lee smiled against his neck. "Sex maniac,"

she whispered, nipping at the tanned skin as she spoke.

"Guilty as charged," Jake growled, entering the bedroom and crossing over to the bed where he lowered her against the beautiful Navajo blanket that served as a spread. He stood staring down at her for a few seconds before turning, his expression unreadable. "I'll be right back, honey."

"Where are you going?" Lee asked, feeling she'd been set adrift, missing the warmth, the feel of his body.

"Only to lock up," Jake told her. "You get beneath the covers before you catch cold," he instructed her as he left the room.

Lee smiled at the authoritative tone in his voice and did as he told her. Most surprising of all, she didn't resent him telling her. And that, she told herself as she settled back against the pillows, is really a giant step forward. *A year ago I'd have come back with some cute remark like "I'm not an idiot, Jake" or "Really, Jake. Must you fuss so?"* She sighed. How true is the old adage that time changes all things.

Sunday was spent taking care of the remaining chores on Jake's list. They replaced several shingles on the roof that had blown off, or rather Jake did, with Lee yelling for him to be careful. Next she watched as Jake split huge blocks of wood into small pieces. Afterward Lee stacked the wood in the small shed to the rear of the cabin.

It was tiring work as they went from one job

141

to another, but Lee didn't mind. She'd look up to find Jake's eyes, dark and unfathomable, watching her. A slow smile would curve the mouth she knew so well, and Lee would positively float on to another chore that awaited her.

She worked relentlessly, her adrenaline pushing her further and further. There was a sense of dread in the back of her mind. But each time she reached for it, sought to grasp the reason for it, its meaning eluded her.

"Well, I guess that's about all we can do for today." Jake's voice broke into the puzzling thoughts plaguing Lee. "I'm afraid it will be several weeks before we can get back up here." He walked over and stood in the opened door of the shed, staring out toward the signs of the inevitable encroachment of winter.

Lee looked up from where she was putting away several hand tools they'd used and the work gloves they'd worn. "Why several weeks?" she asked, disappointment sweeping over her.

Jake turned, a glimmer of understanding in his eyes. "It was only a figure of speech, honey. I'm not sure what my schedule will be and neither are you. Don't worry, we'll come back as soon as we can."

No comment was offered; none was expected. She placed her hand in his outstretched one and followed him from the shed. It occurred to Lee as they covered the short distance to the back door and entered the kitchen that the sense of dread she'd been fighting stemmed from her fear of the days ahead and the regret she felt at having the weekend draw to a close.

CHAPTER NINE

Monday proved to be one of those days that everyone must face sooner or later, a day when all the irritating little things that have been pushed back have to be attended to.

Thus Lee was bound to her desk in the large office allotted the geologists, scribbling away at reports. She knew in her heart that if this were the extent of her job, she'd give it up in a flash.

At that moment the distasteful chore was brought to a temporary halt by the appearance of Diane.

"I know you're just dying to get on with your work, but how about breaking for coffee?" She grinned knowingly, not missing the pleased expression on Lee's face at the suggestion.

"I think you've just saved my sanity," she admitted. Lee came to her feet and grabbed her navy leather purse. "Let's go."

Once seated at a small table in the restaurant close to their office, Lee leaned back and gave a deep sigh of relief. "Honestly, Diane, I can't imagine how you can stand to stay cooped up in that office day in and day out. I'd go stark raving mad."

The redhead grinned. "Simply a matter of preference. I'd be lost on a geological survey, not to mention having to endure the hot sun in summer. Can you possibly imagine the freckles I'd get from such an ordeal?"

Lee shook her head and smiled. "I suppose you're right," she agreed, and changed the subject. "How did your weekend go?"

"So-so. My esteemed boss took me to dinner on Saturday. We even managed to get in a little dancing."

"How nice," Lee drawled, pleased by the news. "Were you able to keep from coming to blows?" she asked teasingly.

"Only barely," Diane admitted somewhat guardedly. "While we were out one of the guys I occasionally date stopped by our table and asked me to dance."

"Did you?" Lee asked eagerly, having no difficulty at all in visualizing Simon's stony features.

"Are you kidding? I hope I'm smarter than that, my dear. As it was Simon glowered for half an hour."

Lee laughed, shaking her head at the explosive relationship. "He's terrible. But I hope you

145

don't give up on him." She watched Diane over the rim of her cup.

"Oh, no!" the other exclaimed dryly. "When he's not in a jealous snit, he's quite lovable. By the way, I called you several times. Was Mark in town?"

"Er, no. That is, I don't think so."

"Oh? Are you seeing someone else?" Diane persisted, not in the least put off by Lee's unwillingness to discuss the subject.

Lee gave her friend a measured look and said, "I spent the weekend with Jake. We drove up to the cabin."

Diane's eyes stretched their widest at this unexpected surprise. "That is fantastic, honey." Her green eyes brimmed with excitement. "Does this mean what I think it does?"

"Perhaps," said Lee. There was a soberness in her expression that wasn't unnoticed by Diane. "We're giving it another try."

"Oh, Lee. I'm so happy for you. It'll work. I just know it will. There's only one thing, though . . ." Diane paused, a knowing look on her face. "What about your job? Has Jake finally relented?"

"Surprisingly enough, he has." Lee laughed as Diane's mouth fell open. "I know how you feel; it caught me the same way. But there are to be no rules, no promises. We'll both simply try as hard as possible."

"Well!" Diane sat back in her chair, stunned. When she'd recovered, she asked, "Are you

146

going to accept any of the jobs coming up? There's one in Texas and another in Oklahoma."

"Certainly," Lee answered crisply. "If our marriage is going to work, then he has to accept that I'm not the ordinary wife. We discussed it."

"And he agreed?" Diane asked incredulously.

"Totally."

"I wonder what made him change his mind?"

That same thought stayed with Lee for the remainder of the coffee break and later as she worked at her desk. Her initial suspicion that Jake was more involved with Sharon Trappe had been put to rest. He'd assured Lee that his interest in that direction was strictly due to his friendship with Sharon's father. Lee believed him. Although in putting that theory to rest she was still left with trying to figure out the reason behind his suggestion that they resume their marriage.

Oh, there was passion between them, a look, a touch, and it totally consumed them, blacking out the entire world. There was also the love they shared. That, too, puzzled Lee as she struggled to make sense out of this latest commitment. How was it possible for two people to still care after the pure hell they'd created for each other?

And yet, in her heart, she knew she would have agreed with Jake's plan even if she'd known that that one weekend would have been it. For no matter how she tried, she was still hopelessly in love with him and always would be.

Then why are you fighting him? her annoying conscience pricked at her. *As Jake pointed out over two years ago, you've proved yourself time and time again as a competent geologist. What is there about you that keeps wanting to inflict pain on yourself as well as Jake?*

Suddenly Lee pushed back the chair she was sitting in and stood. She ran a hand through her blond curls in a gesture of remorse, letting it slide down to cup the cramped muscles of her neck. "Why indeed?" she harshly murmured. "Why indeed?"

The sharp ringing of the telephone sounded and Lee grabbed the receiver as though a lifeline were suddenly dangling before her eyes. "Hello?" she answered, her voice brisk and cool, masking the turmoil within her.

"Lee? How about scooting down to my office? Something's come up with that job down in Lafayette and I need to talk with you," Simon told her.

"I'll be right there, Simon." She cradled the receiver and then paused, a frown crowding her forehead. If she had to go to Louisiana, that meant Jake would be home alone for no telling how many days and nights. Suddenly the idea of being stuck in the bayous for days on end was about as appealing as a mouthful of bilge water!

An hour or so later Lee emerged from Simon's office, a grimly resigned look on her face. At the crack of dawn the following morning, five thirty to be precise, she would find herself on a plane on her way to Lafayette!

She only stopped long enough to go by her office and grab her purse. Simon had given her the rest of the day off to go home and get her packing done.

"How long do you think it will take?" she'd asked Simon as she read through the plug and abandonment sheet filed by previous lessors of the site. Obviously they'd encountered the same problem as Simon's crew, at approximately the same depth. Being a small company, and operating on an exceedingly small budget, they couldn't afford the risk or the expense. They'd given up. Now Lee was faced with finding the problem and deciding if further drilling was advisable.

"Two, three days. I'm not happy with the core samples. We should have reached the lower Tuscaloosa formation by now. I'll give it another week. If you don't find anything that looks promising, we'll pull that rig out."

Somewhere in the back of Lee's mind the idea had been born that she and Jake would have several uninterrupted weeks in which to forge some sort of basis for their marriage, some common ground. She knew Simon had been giving her the lighter work since her accident and she was grateful. Why couldn't he have continued to do so for a little while longer, she wondered miserably.

When Lee let herself into Jake's apartment, which she was now sharing, there wasn't a sound to be heard. She walked through to the kitchen, expecting to see Max busy with the preparation of dinner. Obviously he was out.

Her mood brightened considerably when it occurred to her that Max must have plans of his own for the evening. What better way to greet her husband than over a dinner prepared by her? With renewed eagerness Lee hurried to the bedroom. A quick shower and a change of clothes would do much for her morale. It would also help if she looked her best when she broke the news of her upcoming trip.

The chicken in the deep casserole was simmering nicely amid a thick sauce when Lee added the fresh sliced mushrooms. In separate saucepans on the countertop range were tiny green peas and new potatoes. Fresh spinach salad and crusty rolls rounded out the menu, with plenty of cheese and fruit to finish it off.

Lee darted from the stove to the dining area at one end of the living room. She'd removed all the leaves from the table in order to create the intimate setting she hoped would be present during the meal, but the table still seemed larger than she cared for. Maybe . . . She stood undecided, comparing the small breakfast set in the kitchen to the more elegant one. No. She shook her head. Definitely the dining room. She wanted Jake to see her as the perfect hostess, with candlelight reflected in the lovely gilt-framed mirror that hung over the walnut sideboard, the place settings picture perfect.

There was a breathlessness about Lee as she put the finishing touches to the table, moving a glass forward, a mere touch to the knife and spoon by Jake's plate. She was nervous and it showed.

It occurred to Lee, as she stared down at the chair Jake would sit in, that for the first time in her entire life she was learning what it meant to be concerned with someone's happiness other than her own. Lee wasn't a selfish person, not in the least. But in her childhood struggles against an insensitive mother, and the subsequent years of carefully erecting a protective wall around her true feelings, she'd never been called upon to consider another person's happiness before her own—until Jake. Her inability to give in on the tiniest matter in her marriage had inwardly shaken her.

She'd been taken with Jake from the start, enjoying seeing him stand up to her overbearing mother. She'd gotten a vicarious thrill from knowing she'd thwarted her mother's plans by marrying Jake and having him protect her from her mother's sharp tongue and her periodic attempts at running Lee's life. But to Lee's way of thinking, Jake's surprising demands had been completely unreasonable. In her mind she came to view him as a greater threat than Susan Cramer's annoying interference ever dared to be.

Her miscarriage and Jake's withdrawal

caused the first crack to appear in Lee's carefully built wall of protection. In absorbing that tragedy she didn't find it easy absolving herself of guilt.

Now, through some stroke of fate, she'd been given a second chance. *What if I muff this one as well?* she asked herself. Somehow she had to make Jake see that it was possible to combine her career and her marriage. There just had to be a way.

The sound of a key in the door had Lee catching an unexpected breath and holding it until she thought her chest would explode. Slowly and deliberately she forced herself to relax. After all, she reasoned, she had pointed out the erratic schedule of her job. Surely Jake wouldn't make a scene at this first interruption.

"Well, well," the object of her thoughts said lazily as he entered the living room from the foyer and saw Lee waiting. "Did I forget an important date?" he asked, his dark gaze taking in the attractively set table, the candles, and Lee's pale blue dress of gossamer softness.

He dropped the briefcase he carried on a chair and walked purposefully toward her. His hands reached out and caught the fragile slenderness of her shoulders, drawing her to him. "Whatever the reason, I don't care," he murmured huskily, his lips taking hers in a kiss that had Lee's senses spinning in less time than she cared to admit.

When Jake raised his head, she felt her throat constrict at the warmth emanating from the dark pools staring at her. "Are you pleased?" she whispered. She hated herself for asking, but it was imperative that she gain his fullest approval before bringing up the subject of her trip.

Jake let his hands slide possessively down her back, coming to a halt at the base of her spine, pressing her against the heated warmth of his body. "You know I'm pleased. I've held such a picture in my mind for ages. For a minute—when I first entered—I thought I was dreaming."

"Well, my hardworking husband, if you'll hurry and wash up, you can pour the wine while I serve," she informed him in a sassy manner. Inside she was hating herself for her deceit. Jake's happiness had been genuine and open for the whole world to see. She only wished her own intentions could bear such close scrutiny.

It wasn't enough that he was so open with his approval, he also heaped lavish words of praise on Lee for the superb dinner she'd prepared. Lee accepted the accolades with a smile on her face and a heart as heavy as a brick.

She knew she couldn't put it off any longer. Stubborn and determined she would freely admit to, but deceit . . . that simply wasn't in her makeup.

She picked up the wineglass that Jake had just refilled and raised it to her lips. "I'm afraid this will be our last dinner together for a few days," she announced calmly, watching him over the rim of the glass.

"Oh?" There was no perceptible change in the set of his features or the warmth in his eyes. "Then let's make the most of tonight."

"You . . . you aren't angry?" Lee stuttered, clearly amazed by his calm acceptance.

Jake grinned lazily and leaned back in his chair, one large hand idly toying with his spoon. "I told you, honey, I'm willing to compromise. If you have to go, then"—he shrugged—"that's that."

"I'll have to admit, I'm not looking forward to it," she confessed rather forlornly.

"Come now, Lee. You've worked too hard to give in now. Besides, it won't be forever. Hopefully we'll have the weekend," he told her in a deceptively bland voice.

"What do you mean by hopefully?" she demanded, jumping at once at the slight inference. "Are *you* going to be out of town?" She was unaware of the wistful note creeping into her voice.

"It's turned into a busy week for me. I might be gone tomorrow night, but back by Wednesday afternoon. There's a chance I could be called away Thursday as well. Why? Did you have plans for us?"

"No. No plans. I'd hoped we could go back up to the cabin."

"We'll have to wait and see. However, there is one small problem. I'd planned on having a few people in for dinner Wednesday evening. Do you think you'll be back by then?"

"I'll try, Jake. Do I know any of the people

154

coming?" She struggled to keep a fixed smile on her face in order to hide her disappointment.

He frowned. "I don't think so, other than Sharon Trappe. She'll be with her father, of course. So whatever evil thoughts are stewing in that mean little mind of yours can rest at ease." There was a satisfied gleam of amusement lurking in his warm gaze, almost challenging Lee to disagree.

Unfortunately for Lee it was too much. "Does your former mistress have to come to my home?" she asked icily, glaring at him in an unguarded moment of rage.

"I told you before she isn't, hasn't been, and will never be my mistress, Lee," Jake told her soothingly. "I'm perfectly content with my wife. The Sharon Trappes of this world are the least of my worries. But it's not easy to tell Thomas that he's welcome to have dinner in my home and at the same time exclude his daughter. Don't you agree?"

Lee mulled over the truthfulness of what he'd said. "I suppose so," she mumbled mulishly.

"Good. I'm glad you see it my way." Jake smiled hugely. "Now, let's take the dishes to the kitchen. I'm sure Max won't mind us leaving them this once."

"Where is he, by the way?" Lee asked, getting to her feet at a much slower pace than Jake.

"It's his bowling night."

"Oh, I'd forgotten." She spoke absently, loading the tray and carrying it through to the kitchen. *Damn Simon! Damn that infernal rig in Lafayette! Why couldn't it at least have waited another two days before fouling up?*

"Something wrong, sweetheart?" Jake asked smoothly, too smoothly to suit Lee. And yet he hadn't put a foot wrong the entire evening. His every word, every gesture, had been to praise her, encourage her. So why did she have this gut feeling that she was being laughed at?

That niggling fixation stayed with Lee during the evening and through the night. Even the next morning, when Jake insisted on taking her to the airport, she found herself watching him, alert to the tiniest flaw in his behavior that could account for her unease.

When her flight was announced, Lee looked up at Jake, a wealth of love in the depths of her blue eyes. Instead of telling him she loved him, telling him that she'd rather stay home with him, she said, "Don't forget to pick up Tom from the vet's. And, oh, yes, would you mind speaking to my landlord? I'm sure I'll have to pay something for breaking my lease. I'll finish packing my things when I get back." God, but she sounded cool and confident—and she wasn't, not at all.

"Don't worry," Jake assured her, pushing the magazines he'd bought for her into her hands and guiding her through the crowd. "Max and I will take care of everything. You just concentrate on finishing that job and get back to me."

"I will, Jake, I will." She came to a sudden stop, causing Jake to do the same, staring questioningly at her. Lee stood on tiptoe and kissed him, her slender arms hugging him close. "I love you, Jake," she whispered, and then hurried away.

CHAPTER TEN

The time in flight was sufficient for Lee to examine the conflicting emotions she was experiencing. She'd set Jake up, or so she'd imagined, plying him with delicious food, good wine, candlelight—the whole schmear—and then let her little bomb fall.

Instead of the storm she'd been expecting, he'd shown no more reaction than if she'd said she was going shopping for the day.

Face it, she thought scowlingly, *you wanted him to react, if not violently, then at least angrily, and for what?*

Was there some deep-rooted desire within her that wanted her marriage to fail? Was her acquiescence in the resumption of their marriage merely a foil, covering up a secret desire to see Jake hurt?

Both thoughts, while disturbing, were dismissed. Her love for Jake ran too deep for her to take seriously such Freudian hang-ups. What was really pulling at her was the encouragement he'd given her, repeating, she remembered, almost the exact same words she'd hurled at him on their honeymoon, such as her struggles, her fight to get to the top. Never in her wildest dreams had she thought those same words would haunt her.

Lee stared remorsefully out the window of the huge jet, seeing nothing, hearing nothing. *Is this all there is to it? Will I always be flying hither and yon while Jake enjoys the comforts of home? Is this really what I want?*

She gave herself a mental jerk, breaking the painful introspection. She was amazed with herself and the continuing doubts flooding her mind. Instead of worrying over Jake's reaction to her trip, it struck Lee that she should be rejoicing. She'd fought him for three long years in order to have her way. Now that she'd won, the logical thing to do was savor the victory.

By the time the plane landed in Baton Rouge, Lee's thoughts were, for the most part, calm and settled. Any annoying flashbacks that managed to slip through were immediately submerged. She'd trained herself to put personal problems aside, refusing to allow them to infringe on the job at hand—her performance.

After claiming her one piece of luggage, Lee quickly located the car rental booths. A short time later, armed with a map plus directions from the hospitable clerk, Lee found herself heading west along Interstate 10.

It was a lonely drive, the overcast skies combined with the skeletal starkness of the cypress trees that flanked the highway; their limbs laden with Spanish moss gave one an eerie feeling. It brought to mind the haunting sadness of Longfellow's poem and the star-crossed lovers, Gabriel and Evangeline. On another day, in a better frame of mind, Lee was sure she could enjoy the gentle mood of the bayou country. At the moment, however, it only seemed to remind her of Jake, hundreds of miles away from her.

At Lafayette Lee turned south and drove a short distance and then took highway 96 toward St. Martinville. She'd gone only about seven miles when she saw the markers indicating the Garrett Exploration site.

By the time Lee had covered the mile or so of little more than a rutted track, she was convinced that every tooth in her head, and every bone in her body, had been jarred loose. She parked the car alongside several trucks of various sizes, the exterior of each covered with the same black mud she'd just driven through.

She opened the door and got out, reaching back inside the car for the heavy briefcase containing the more pertinent data regarding the well, and for her large shoulder-strap bag. Her face wore a grim expression as she made her way across the damp, sticky ground toward the trailer that sat to the right of the drilling platform.

God, she thought as she finally reached a wooden platform of sorts. *What a depressing location!* She turned and looked toward the drill site, the frame towering over the trees. A ghost of a smile tugged at her lips as she encountered the curious stares of the crew—a situation she'd become immune to over the years.

One man in particular had seen her arrival and hurried toward her, a smile on his leathery cheeks.

"Lee!" he shouted, his voice carrying over the roar of the huge generators. "This is a nice surprise." He grasped her hand in his large calloused one and dropped a light peck on her forehead. This action was met with a series of hoots and shrill whistles from the crew.

"Hello, Mike. I hear you've got some problems," she remarked, ignoring their audience.

Mike Jensen was tops in his field, and a very nice man besides. Lee had worked with him before and was looking forward to doing so again. Contrary to some of the other men she'd come in contact with along the way, Mike accepted her findings with complete confidence. She'd learned after their first job together that he was the proud father of two daughters. One was enrolled in medical school, and the other was a recent graduate with a law degree. Since then Lee had felt a kindred spirit with the middle-aged man, loving his brisk manner and his salty language.

"I tell you, honey," he responded, holding open the door of the trailer for her, "that damn

161

thing"—he hooked one thumb toward the platform—"has worried the flaming hell out of me. I know there's oil down there, but short of a damn volcanic eruption, I don't see how we're going to get at it."

Lee couldn't help but smile as she listened to him. She placed her things on the large desk, in a spot cleared for her by Mike, and turned to face him. "Don't you know that at your age you shouldn't get so excited? It's not good."

Mike removed his hard-hat, tossing it toward a couch of questionable vintage, and frowned. "Have you added therapy to your list of accomplishments?" he snorted, taking down two thick, serviceable mugs and filling them with coffee.

"No, you old grouch, but it wouldn't hurt you to listen," Lee shot back, accepting the mug and raising it to her lips. "Ugh!" she exclaimed as soon as she tasted the coffee. "That's horrible."

"Ahh . . ." He chuckled. "I can see you haven't developed a taste for chicory."

"Indeed I haven't," she spluttered, marching over to the sink and emptying the contents of the mug down the drain.

"Well, if you feel that way about it, you can try this." He handed her a jar of the instant variety.

"Thanks," Lee muttered, eyeing him narrowly as she measured the proper amount. "Is there any hot water?" she asked sourly. "Or am I supposed to mix it with something?"

"Right behind you on the counter." He nodded toward the electric percolator. "I keep that for those unappreciative of real coffee."

"In a pig's eye!" Lee scorned. "No wonder you're having trouble with this hole. That darn brew has addled your brain."

Mike merely chuckled. He hooked a chair with one booted foot and motioned Lee to sit. "How's it been going with you?" he asked, carefully lowering his large frame into a much stouter-made seat. "Have you completely recovered from your little fiasco in Kuwait?"

"Yes. Although I think it's left me rather leery of going there again."

"I know the feeling. I did a five-year stint over there once. I've never seen the like for fighting and fussing. One minute everything's as peaceful as can be. The next thing you know they're yelling and screaming like a bunch of damn idiots. It makes it difficult for the officials to keep order," Mike observed knowingly.

They chatted for a while longer, lingering over their coffee before getting down to work. Mike showed Lee the problem facing them, shaking his head in disgust.

"I can't figure it out, Lee. There's a lot of tension on the drill and we're losing too much mud."

Lee studied the information before her, including the electrologs, sidewall core logs, and the gamma ray logs. The core samples for the last few days were indeed puzzling. All logical reasoning pointed to the fact that they should be well within the lower Tuscaloosa formation by now. But the samples certainly disclaimed this assumption.

"According to the abandonment sheet filed by the previous company, they encountered a similar problem," Lee pointed out as the two of them scanned numerous data and graphs.

It was comparable to looking for the proverbial needle in the haystack. You knew the solution was there; the problem was finding it.

By late afternoon Lee was fairly certain she'd come up with something. If her calculations proved correct, she could be on her way back to Denver within hours. She put the suggestion to Mike, backed up with what she hoped she'd found.

"Well, I'll be damned," he grunted musingly. "A dang fault." He looked at Lee, a thoughtful expression in his eyes. "That would account for the tension on the drill."

"Correct. Instead of going through the Pluxzy Zone and into the Lower Tuscaloosa formation, the drill has become wedged in this fault." Lee pointed to what she considered the problem. "Obviously this is the same thing that stopped the other company."

"What do you suggest we do?"

"I'd bring the drill back up and angle it"— she did some fast figuring—"at a two-degree angle southwest of the southwest extremity. We should know fairly soon if that approach will bypass the fault."

* * *

Several hours later found Lee once again at the airport in Baton Rouge, with barely enough time to turn in the rental car and check her luggage. It had been a close squeeze, making the drive in time to catch the flight to Dallas, and then on to Denver.

Mike had been surprised when she refused to wait until morning. "Are you sure you want to go tonight?"

"I'm positive, Mike. I'd like to be back in Denver as soon as possible."

He shook his head. "You remind me of my own girls. They think nothing of going off on their own at any hour of the day or night. I guess I'm old-fashioned, but I like to think of my woman waiting for me, not the other way around."

"You're not alone in that opinion, Mike," Lee grimly replied.

The flight was smooth and uneventful, for which Lee was grateful. All she needed at this point was to be involved in some freaky hijacking or, worse, for Jake to wash his hands of her.

It was a little before midnight when Lee let herself into the apartment. She hurried through the living room, surprised to find a lamp still on. Perhaps Max had been doing some late-night reading. As she entered the master bedroom she could hear the shower running in the adjoining bath.

A shaft of relief ran through her. Jake *was* at home. She dropped the suitcase to the floor and slipped her tired feet from her shoes. The fatigue that had been like a weight across her shoulders suddenly left her. She'd hoped, but knowing how busy he was, she hadn't really expected him to be home.

She stood in the middle of the floor, not certain how to go about greeting her husband. Should she rush in and surprise him in the shower or simply wait until he came out?

For some inexplicable reason, she found herself suffering from a severe case of nerves. There was also a hint of shyness where Jake was concerned. And yet she had done everything humanly possible to get back to him—back to the warmth of his love, his embrace. *I think I must be cracking up,* she thought for one hysterical moment. *I'm beginning to question every single thing I do.*

Just at that moment the shower was turned off and Lee heard the quiet swoosh as the door was pushed back. Before she could decide what course of action to take, Jake appeared in the doorway. His face and head were hidden by the large towel he was briskly rubbing his hair with; the rest of his body was completely naked.

Lee couldn't find it in her to speak, her gaze drawn to the powerful, virile image of him as he stood in total unawareness that he was being observed. Her eyes ran the compelling course of his tall frame, eagerly, hungrily reveling in the knowledge of possession. He belonged to her. In that instant she knew she would do anything to keep him.

Whether from the very quietness of the room

or sensing the presence of another person near him, Jake's hands stilled their movement, the towel sliding from his face. He stared at Lee, a slow smile working its way from his curving mouth to crinkle the tiny network of lines at the corners of his dark eyes.

"How long have you been here?" he rasped huskily, dropping the towel on the floor and holding out his arms.

"Only a few minutes," Lee whispered and closed the space between them with a rush. "Oh, Jake," she sighed brokenly. "I was so afraid you'd be away."

Instead of replying, Jake caught her chin in one hand and raised her head, his mouth going unerringly to hers in a bruising kiss.

Lee welcomed the harshness of the on-slaught, her tongue, no longer tentative and shy, meeting his daringly.

She was still caught up in the strange new-ness of knowing this man was hers. It never occurred to her that she was thinking in a man-ner that had annoyed her when expressed by Jake so often in the past.

Her hands that had been caught against Jake's chest now wiggled free and began to ca-ress the tanned back and shoulders, kneading, rubbing, unable to get enough of him.

Jake reluctantly drew his mouth hers, his eyes like dark embers. "T thing wrong here," he murmur unbuttoning her blouse. Lee f remain still as he undressed her. There was an urgency in his movements, and this excited her.

Without another word between them, they moved to the bed and into each other's arms. Jake at once lowered his body over Lee's, his taking of her swift and vital. There was a gasp of pleasure from Lee, her arms grasping him and hugging him close. Whispered words of endearment rushed unthinkingly from her lips. She was like someone who had been deprived of a life-saving elixir; her need was insatiable.

Jake, sensing her mood, accelerated his love-making to a tension-paced pattern that led Lee along a course unlike any other she'd ever experienced. There were no words to describe the endless moments. She clung to him with all her strength as he carried her through the most primitive of passions between a man and woman. When the final explosive wave rushed over them, Jake held Lee in a powerful grasp, her name breaking from deep within his throat, thrown into the bottomless void that swirled around them.

It was a long time before Lee could bring herself to move. Even the opening of her eyes seemed to require Herculean strength. Jake's head was resting on her breasts, one muscled leg thrown over her slim thighs. In a slow, almost druglike effort, she raised one hand and let it rest on the still damp crispness of the dark head, savoring the feel, the rush of love that stole over her.

Jake stirred under the gentle caress, propping

himself up on one elbow, his chin on his fist. He stared down at the pink fullness of his wife's lips, the blue eyes turned dark from passion, the flush of lovemaking still present in her cheeks. "If this is the sort of homecoming I can look forward to each time you're away, would you please plan your next trip soon?" he murmured throatily.

Lee stared back, feeling the heat of his gaze as it slowly made its way over her body. "What if I don't want to go away again?" The question surprised her even more than Jake. Why on earth had she said such a thing?

"I'd think it wonderful, but we both know that's not likely to happen, don't we?" Jake remarked without undo concern. "How did you manage to get back so quickly?" As he spoke one hand began to slide over the taut firmness of her stomach and upward to idly trace a rosy tip to erection.

"I was lucky." Lee smiled, and told him what had gone wrong and her suggestions that had worked. "I was rather proud of myself. Are you pleased that I was able to get back tonight?"

"What do you think?" Jake growled, bending his head and flicking the erect nipple with the tip of his moist tongue.

"Jake!" Lee closed her eyes against the traitorous desire leaping in her veins. "Stop. How can I carry on an intelligent conversation with you if you do that?"

He gave a final tug with his lips and drew back, a look of mock sternness in his eyes.

"Hasn't it occurred to you by now that I'm far more interested in making love to you than talking?" He buried his face in the hollow of her neck and shoulder and nipped the tip of a pink earlobe in punishment.

"Ouch!" Lee squeaked, squirming against him. "That hurt me, you brute."

"I meant it to. You need to improve your timing. I don't like being interrupted." He spoke softly against her hair.

"Please, Jake. Just this once?" She twisted her body around so that she was facing him. "It didn't seem to matter one way or the other when I told you I might not be going away again. Why?"

Jake gave a deep sigh of resignation and dropped onto his back. The look he subjected Lee to was thoughtful and searching, leaving her to wonder at its meaning. "If I didn't know better, I would suspect you of trying to start an argument."

"Don't be ridiculous," she said very carefully. "Why would I want to do that?" Her gaze dropped to stare somewhere in the region of his chest, unable to brave the truthfulness of what he'd said. For it was true—and for the life of her, Lee couldn't understand the letdown she was experiencing.

"I think it's something you're going to have to work out for yourself, honey. If I were to tell you, you'd resent it."

Lee pouted. "Thanks loads. You make me sound like some sort of nut."

Jake gathered her to him, his arms holding her close. "I'm sorry if I gave that impression, sweetheart, for that's not how I see you at all. I do, however, think that you're emotionally involved in a struggle that no one can help you with."

For a moment Lee thought over the gist of his remark, not at all pleased. She wanted, no, needed, something more from him. She pushed his arms away and struggled into a sitting position. "Why do you insist on speaking in riddles, Jake?" she asked sharply, a frown clouding her features.

"What are you mad about, Lee? Are you annoyed that I haven't raised hell over the trip you took today? That I haven't demanded that you devote all your time to me?" he asked blandly. "If that's the case, then I'm afraid you're in for a disappointment. Whatever we give to this marriage will be given freely or not at all."

Lee knew there was logic in his statement, but she wasn't in the mood for logic or common sense or any other form of rational thinking. She glared at Jake from beneath her thick lashes. How could she break through that calm facade, prod him into declaring himself? She didn't care for this attitude of indifference, didn't care for it at all! Besides, with her flying all over the country, he was fair game for any woman he met.

"There's one subject we've avoided," she said

deliberately. "How about children? Do you still consider me such a bad risk?"

Jake didn't answer immediately. It was as though he were carefully considering her question. "First of all, I do not consider you a . . . bad risk . . . as you put it. The blame for the miscarriage, if there is any blame, was as much my fault as yours. I pushed you into a situation you weren't ready to accept." He saw the suspicious brightness of tears in her eyes and stared fixedly at her. "Are you laboring under the misguided thought that you caused the miscarriage by refusing to give up your career?" he asked sharply.

Lee nodded, raising tortured eyes to meet his. "It has occurred to me on occasion," she answered meekly, for the first time admitting to the feelings of guilt she'd suffered these past few months.

"Then put that damn fool notion out of your head, baby," Jake growled, moving with surprising swiftness to hook an arm around her middle and haul her back against him. When he'd settled her into the curve of his huge frame, he said, "I talked with the doctor at length and he assured me that even if you'd wrapped yourself in cotton, you'd have had trouble. It wasn't your fault, and I'll be damned if I'll stand by and allow you to blame yourself."

The gentle roughness of his voice, his large hands brushing the hair from her face, was like a catharsis, cleansing her of the guilt that had lain so heavily on her conscience.

"Why didn't you ever mention this?" Jake asked.

"I suppose I was too afraid of what you'd say," she whispered against the tanned column of his neck. "You have no idea how the expressions that were mirrored in your face the day you visited me in the hospital hurt me. They were expressions I wasn't capable of dealing with. And later, combined with my own inadequacies, the guilt became more than I could deal with . . . I couldn't push it back and forget it. I suppose I let it take over my emotions."

"And now?"

"Now we're talking . . . discussing, trying to make our marriage work. It just seemed important for me to know how you felt."

"Right now I'm feeling very lucky," Jake mused wickedly, "and I think I'll make love to my wife again."

Since Lee found no fault with this delightful suggestion, she was very helpful as he proceeded to do just that.

CHAPTER ELEVEN

Morning found Lee up early and in the kitchen with Max as they went over the plans for the dinner that evening. Rather, Max told her his plans for the menu and Lee agreed. There was no reason not to, and she was wise enough to realize this.

She ran down the list of things needed for the festivities that Max had given her. "Are you sure there isn't anything you've forgotten?" she asked thoughtfully, adding a couple of items of her own.

"I think we've covered it all. The flowers and the table I'll leave to you." He grinned. "Arranging delicate posies isn't my strong suit."

"Nonsense, Max. I've always thought your arrangements were very nicely done." Lee defended the burly man without looking up. "Let's see now," she murmured. "I called

Marta and she's having lunch with me. I'm going to the hairdresser's. I'll take care of your shopping and pick up the flowers."

"That about does it," Max said as he refilled their cups with coffee. "By the way, it sure is nice having you back."

"Thanks, Max. I must admit I'm rather pleased myself. Oh, by the way. If anyone from my office calls today, tell them I'm, er, taking some time off."

"Make a note of that, Max," Jake remarked from the doorway. He was wearing a short navy velour robe, and Lee had an idea that was all. His face still bore the shadowy growth of beard, and his dark hair was tousled. He yawned hugely, then walked over and sat down next to Lee. "Do you two earlybirds realize that it's not even seven o'clock yet?" he growled, frowning, nodding his thanks as Max set a steaming cup of coffee before him.

"Please drink your coffee, Jake, before you try to engage in the *gentle* art of conversation." Lee regarded him humorously.

"One more crack from you, young lady, and I'll turn you across my knee," he said silkily. He raised the cup and half-emptied its contents in one swallow.

"Promises, promises," Lee murmured teasingly in his ear as she touched her lips to his scratchy cheek and then jumped to her feet and out of his reach as he made a grab for her. "More coffee, Max. Your boss is definitely in a foul mood this morning."

"Where are you off to?" Jake asked, eyeing the way the soft material of the blue robe hugged Lee's figure, the tousled disarray of her hair.

"After I shower and dress I've a list of errands to run for Max and some of my own. Why?" she asked. "Did you want me for something?"

Instead of answering, Jake simply held her gaze, her innocently spoken question bringing a blush to her cheeks as she read the open invitation in his eyes.

"Why are you playing hookey from the office?" he finally asked, breaking the spell by which he'd held her imprisoned.

"Do I have to have a reason? I have some time coming, so I decided to take today off. Do you object?" she asked archly.

"Oh, no, I'm just surprised, that's all."

Not any more than I am, Lee thought confusedly as she left the kitchen and hurried to get her shower. Quite frankly, nothing made sense these days, other than the time spent with Jake. She paused in the bedroom on her way to the shower, glancing toward the king-size bed and remembering the wild abandonment with which she'd returned Jake's lovemaking the night before. It suddenly hit her that she was staying home because she wanted to. Garrett Exploration could strike oil in the middle of Times Square and it wouldn't matter to her!

Good heavens! She drew a shaky breath as she slipped out of her robe. *I think I've fallen*

*head over heels in love with my husband all over
again.* Only this time she had no desire to leave
him. In fact, were it possible, she'd climb into
his hip pocket and never be apart from him.

The realization was sobering. Lee had always
dealt with facts, things that could be seen, be
proven. She wasn't one to leave things to
chance. Yet, here she was, her world turned
upside down, and she couldn't figure out when
or how it had happened. It was disconcerting.
Worst of all, she had a sneaky suspicion that
Jake also knew.

She'd been had and by a master. But instead
of feeling angry at Jake, she knew a wealth of
love that was immeasurable, knew that it was
his caring, his refusal to admit defeat, that had
brought about this chance at love for them.

It was with a sigh of relief that Lee sank into
the chair opposite Marta in the restaurant several hours later. "Wow! I'm bushed," she greet-
ed her sister, who was as radiant as a bride.

"What on earth have you been doing?"
Marta laughed.

"Running errands . . . and more errands,"
Lee grinned. "How's the romance coming
along?"

"Since you just happened to ask . . ." Her
sister smiled. She raised her left hand and held
it conspicuously before her mouth in a feigned
yawn, the fingers straight and stiff.

"Marta!" Lee exclaimed, leaning forward excitedly. "Are my eyes deceiving me, or is that

a wedding band on the appropriate finger of your left hand?"

"Yes," the new bride laughingly admitted. "Didn't you wonder when you called me at Jim's apartment?"

"Frankly, no. I just assumed you were, er, staying with him," Lee admitted, rather embarrassed. "But wait a minute. Why wasn't I invited to the wedding?"

"Would you believe it? We eloped." Marta chuckled. "Poor Jim. I'm not sure he'll ever recover from the indignity of skulking off like two errant teenagers."

"How did Mother take the news?" Lee asked curiously.

"Please!" Marta momentarily closed her eyes against the horrible scene that had taken place. "She was livid. And, as you predicted, she used every trick in the book, from a sudden and mysterious heart condition to the usual rot about sacrificing her life for me." She shuddered. "I'm afraid I saw a side of her that I would have been just as happy not knowing about."

"Put it behind you, Marta," Lee wisely advised. "You gave her enough years of your life. Our mother is the original iron maiden when it comes to getting her way."

"Oh, Lee. I wish . . . it doesn't—"

"I know, I know," Lee interrupted. "You'd like for us to be a normal, happy family. Perhaps we will be someday. At the moment, however, I'm afraid there's little chance of that happening. Not only have you gone and ruined Mother's chances of having a celebrity for a daughter, but I've added to her misery."

Marta's curiosity was halted with the approach of the waiter to take their orders. Once he was gone she looked across at Lee. "What have you done?" The anxiety in her voice was not lost on her younger and much stronger sister.

"Jake and I are back together." Lee announced simply. She leaned back in her chair and watched in an amused fashion as poor Marta struggled to cope with the stunning news.

"I can't believe it." Suddenly there appeared a mischievous gleam in her eyes. "Have *you* told Mother?" They both laughed. "Seriously, though, you know I'm pleased. I had an idea something was in the works when he left for London. I've never seen a man in a worse state."

They talked on, savoring the new relationship that had sprung up between them, plus making plans to have dinner and give their husbands a chance to get to know each other.

By the time they'd finished eating, Lee knew she'd never again allow her mother to come between her and her sister. Marta was too gentle a person to stand up to Susan Cramer. However, Lee had no trouble in doing so, and she had an idea that Jim wouldn't hesitate to set his mother-in-law straight. From what she'd heard of her new brother-in-law, he was exactly what

Marta needed, strength tempered with kindness and love.

It was with a sense of well-being that Lee left the restaurant and headed for Jake's office, two blocks away. She'd deliberately budgeted her time in order to have the extra thirty minutes or so for a surprise visit with her husband.

I'm acting like a silly teenager, she thought with a wry twist of her mouth as she swung along, a spring in her step. But she didn't care. She felt like someone who had been given a new lease on life, a reprieve from an existence that promised only loneliness and a surfeit of bittersweet memories.

Rose Graves masked her surprise as Lee entered the office, a warm smile of greeting curving her generous mouth. "Lee, how nice to see you."

"Hello, Rose. You're looking lovely, as usual," she remarked, and meant it. Had she been ten years younger, Lee often wondered if she would have approved so easily of Jake's choice of secretaries. "Still guarding the holy of holies?" Lee teased, coming to a halt at the corner of the desk and leaning against the dark wood.

"Of course." She grinned conspiratorially. "That's the main reason for the exorbitant salary your husband pays me." The brunette cast a furtive glance toward the closed door of Jake's office and back to Lee. "Did Jake know you were going to stop by?"

"No," Lee slowly answered, not missing Rose's slight agitation. "I have a few minutes to spare before my appointment at the hairdresser's, so I decided to surprise him. Is he busy?" she asked curiously.

"Er, you could call it that," the secretary remarked, her voice tinged with annoyance.

"Oh? Anyone I know?"

"I'm not sure. It's Sharon Trappe. She swept through here about ten minutes ago and was in Jake's office before I could stop her."

"I see," Lee muttered ominously. She straightened from her lounging position, a murderous glint in her blue eyes. "I think I'll give Miss Trappe a dose of her own medicine, Rose. I don't at all care for her being alone with my husband." She placed an unconscious emphasis on the last two words which did not go undetected by the older woman.

"That sounds like a marvelous idea," Rose replied to the rigidly set back and shoulders of Lee as she strode purposefully toward Jake's office, her hand grasping the handle.

Inwardly Lee was seething! If Jake wanted to play footsie with Sharon Trappe, then he damn well would have to tell her to her face.

A sixth sense warned her against flinging open the door, causing her instead to let the weight of the heavy panel carry it back.

The two people in the large, graciously appointed office were unaware of Lee's presence. They were standing in front of the wide, sweeping windows that took over one entire wall of the room, their backs angled toward the door.

Sharon was pressing her diminutive figure against Jake, her face lifted enticingly to his.

Lee stood, an angered paralysis gripping her entire body as the sultry sound of the brunette's voice could be heard in her not at all subtle attempt at persuasion.

"You know how it will be, darling. Your wife can't be bothered with taking care of you or your home. And really, Jake, you must admit it's not very romantic making love to a woman who smells like she's been working on an oil rig." She tried to add an extra edge to her campaign by reaching up with one scarlet-tipped hand to clasp Jake's neck.

Instead of the response Lee was almost certain he would make, Jake caught Sharon's hand and removed it. He stepped back and said, "You're making this unnecessarily difficult, Sharon. Even if I didn't love Lee, I wouldn't be interested in continuing our relationship." The bluntness of his admission shocked Lee with its cruelness. "As for my wife, we've worked our problems out very nicely. I've no qualms whatsoever with our arrangements."

"I don't believe that, darling." Sharon continued her bitter attack. "You're only talking like this because you feel some sort of misguided loyalty to that ridiculous tomboy you're tied to. Let her have her stupid career; I'll make you forget about her, you'll see." The dulcet tones of inducement dripped from her honeyed voice.

Lee didn't wait for Jake's reply. She transferred her hand to the edge of the door and slammed it with resounding force. Both figures by the window swung round at the sound. For a moment Lee was struck by the humor of the moment.

Sharon's face was suffused with color, her eyes narrowed in a blast of fury. Jake, on the other hand, was surprisingly calm. He caught the light of battle in Lee's icy blue stare and grinned.

"Hello, sweetheart. Is something wrong or were you just dying to see me?" He walked over to where Lee was standing and slipped an assuring arm around her waist, dropping a light kiss on her cheek at the same time. "I believe you've met Sharon?"

"Oh, yes. She came by your apartment the day after we got back from London," Lee said dismissively, utter contempt revealed in the look she leveled toward Jake's guest. "Perhaps I should inform your . . . friend that I've no intention of divorcing you, dahling," she mimicked, using Sharon's drawling pronunciation of the word, "and more important, that you haven't asked to be released from our marriage."

Sharon subjected Lee to a withering scrutiny, her hands clenched into tight fists. "Everyone knows your preference for chasing about the world while you leave your husband to fend for himself. You've made him a laughingstock among his friends."

Lee's chin rose to a haughty angle, her expression one of chilly disdain. "I think, Miss

Trappe, you're the laughingstock. Your ridiculous pursuit of *my* husband has been the topic of more than a few conversations, believe me. If I were you, I'd seriously consider a lengthy vacation. Perhaps Acapulco, the Bahamas? But before you go, let me give you a word of advice. Make sure the next man you start chasing is single. Another wife might not be as open-minded as I've been."

"Why you—"

"Don't press your luck," Lee took a menacing step forward, only to be stopped by Jake's restraining arm around her waist.

Sharon rushed toward the door, nervously edging past Lee. "The two of you deserve each other," she flung over her shoulder as she gained the safety of the door, slamming it shut behind her.

The silence stretched interminably in the room after Sharon's climactic exit, or so it seemed to Lee. She couldn't quite bring herself to face Jake. Her jealousy had left her feeling strangely vulnerable, unsure of his reaction. She stood meekly by his side, castigating herself for her behavior, waiting for Jake to break the bone-chilling silence, when suddenly she became aware that his body was shaking.

Troubled blue eyes slowly inched upward over gray tweed shoulders, crisp white collar, and conservative blue and gray striped tie, to encounter the warm, brown orbs of her husband, their depths brimming with laughter.

"Oh, honey," he laughed, "you were magnificent. I'm not sure my ego will ever return to its normal size." He jerked her to him, his face muffled against the scented softness of her hair. "God, Lee! I do love you," he murmured huskily.

"I know, Jake, I know," she whispered, her own voice strangely constricted.

Finally he eased her back, his features taut with the emotion-filled moment. "Thank you for not jumping to the conclusion that I was carrying on with Sharon."

"I was ready to fight for you, Jake," she admitted unashamedly. "I've always known I loved you, but now I know that I can't live without you."

"Then there's no problem, is there? I've realized that same thing for a long time now. I'd have agreed to almost anything to get you back. I find myself totally without pride where you're concerned." Before Lee knew what was happening, Jake swooped her up in his arms and strode around the desk and sank into the large leather chair. "Now"—he smiled disarmingly —"would you care to heap more words of praise on my head?"

"No, you conceited devil," Lee remarked dryly, squirming until her body was neatly tucked into the curve of his. "I can see now that I've greatly erred."

"Don't you believe it," Jake drawled, his hands sliding seductively over her rounded hips, slender waist, and thrusting breasts.

"Who knows, I just might become an outrageous flirt, merely to see my beautiful wife guard me so zealously."

"Zealous, my foot! You are an ungrateful lout. What you'll get is a rap over the head with Max's largest iron skillet." She eyed him balefully. " 'Tis a very short leash you'll be on from now on, me laddie, very short indeed." Her blue eyes sparkled lovingly.

Jake stared at her, unable to believe his luck. "Somehow I don't mind the sentence at all. The jailer has such . . . interesting ways of entertaining me. Speaking of which, would you care to go home right now and begin my punishment?"

"You're insatiable," Lee murmured against the sensual curve of the lips nipping at hers. "But I can't, I have a hairdresser's appointment in ten minutes."

"Damn the hairdresser!" Jake thundered, taking her lips in a savage kiss that left Lee floundering in a rush of desire.

It was a shaky Jake who broke the embrace, his breathing reduced to ragged gasps. He let his head fall against the high back of the chair, his eyes dulled with passion. "How would you like to have me make love to you here and now?"

Lee smiled the lazy smile of a woman sure of herself and her lover. "You wanted to have a dinner party. Have you forgotten?"

"No, damn it, I haven't forgotten. I'll probably be the first host ever to ask his guests to leave before dessert is served."

"You wouldn't dare?"

"Would you care if I did?

"Not in the least."

"Good. Because I very well might do just that," he threatened darkly. "And now"—he pushed back a white cuff—"I think you'd better scoot."

"Will you be home early?" Lee asked, coming to her feet and pulling her clothes straight.

"I think you know the answer to that," Jake remarked ruefully, lying back in the chair, enjoying the sight of her.

Lee bent and retrieved her purse from beneath the edge of the desk. As she straightened, she gave Jake a meaningful look. "Remember one thing, Jake Rhome. You're my own personal tom cat, and as such you'll prowl only in my bedroom. Understood?"

"Yes, ma'am."

"Good. See you at five thirty."

On leaving the beauty shop an hour later, Lee knew there was one more stop to add to her list. She hoped Simon would understand.

Lee stood beside Jake as they said good night to the last of their guests. When the door finally closed, they looked at each other and smiled.

"I was so disappointed that Sharon wasn't able to be here," Lee drawled sweetly as she began picking up the remaining glasses scattered about the living room and headed toward the kitchen.

"Oh, I'm sure you were devastated," Jake

snorted, following close behind. "I could tell you were really broken up."

"That's the last of it, Max," Lee said, popping the glasses into the dishwasher. "Why don't you call it a night. We can tackle the rest of the cleaning in the morning."

"I think I will," Max agreed, falling in with her suggestion with an alacrity that surprised Jake.

Later, in their bedroom, Jake remarked that Max must not be feeling well.

"Oh? What makes you say that?" she asked.

"I've never known him to go to bed early. Ever since I met him, he's been a regular night owl."

"Well, if you're really worried, we'll have him see a doctor," Lee said. She turned to find Jake staring at her, his hands busily unbuttoning his shirt.

"I have a sneaky suspicion that I'm being had. What's going on?"

"Oh, you're impossible," she frowned. "Max knows I have something to tell you. I imagine this is his way of making sure we aren't disturbed."

As soon as the words were out of her mouth, Jake became perfectly still, clad only in his well-fitting trousers, his gaze shuttered. "What do you have to tell me that would cause Max to scurry to his room like a timid mouse?"

Lee walked over to her suddenly storm-featured husband and slipped her arms around his waist. "I had a talk with Simon today. I'm now a part-time geologist!"

When there was no response to her announcement, she repeated it, a frown marring the smoothness of her brow. "Did you hear me, Jake?"

"I'm not sure. I thought you said you now have a part-time job. Does this mean what I think it does?" His features grew taut as he reached out and grabbed the slenderness of her shoulders. "Don't play with me about this, Lee. If you're not sure about it, then don't make rash promises."

"But I am sure, Jake," she cried, begging him to believe with her voice, her eyes. "I spent the most miserable day of my life yesterday on that oil rig. All I could think about was you, here in this bed, this apartment. It almost drove me crazy to think you might be away when I got back." She nodded her head. "Oh, yes, Jake, I'm sure. I've accomplished what I set out to do."

"And now?" he quietly asked.

"And now I want to devote more of my time to you."

Jake continued to watch her, the hooded, searching gaze seeming to bore into her very soul. "You do realize that you can't play with this decision like a child choosing a toy, don't you? What happens if you suddenly become bored?"

"I don't think that's likely to happen, do you? It'll give me the best of both worlds." Her blue eyes darkened as she remembered the nights spent in this room, in his arms.

"There'll be no going back," he repeated.

"I know that. But this time is different. You didn't try to *make* me change my mind. You accepted me as I was, Jake. By doing that you made me see that loving someone brings with it a special sort of caring."

For the first time the beginnings of a roguish grin touched his mouth. "Does this special caring include warning off other women as you did today?" The hands on her shoulders began a gentle kneading, inching downward until they encountered the softness of her buttocks.

"Most definitely," Lee whispered in an indrawn gasp as Jake pulled her against the heated arousal of his thighs. Suddenly he tired of the barrier of clothing that kept her body hidden from his gaze. He found the zipper at the back of the sexy green dress and brought it down none too gently. The sheer panty hose were dealt with in the same careless manner.

When Jake would have moved them both toward the bed, Lee stopped him. "Ah, no, Mr. Rhome. I'm a liberated lady, remember? I also get as much pleasure in seeing your body as you do from mine." With a deftness and a kinder regard for his clothes, Lee lost little time in removing the last garment from his tanned body.

By then Jake's restraint was at an end. He reached for Lee with a groan and carried her to the bed, where they both fell in a heated tangle of arms and legs. There was an eagerness in their caresses as hands went unerringly to familiar places of arousal, to hidden secrets that opened, warm and moist, to exploring fingers.

The heat of their passion flowed around them, holding them prisoners in its powerful grasp, as each parry and thrust brought them closer to the ultimate consummation of their love.

"I love you, Jake," Lee whispered hoarsely, her body writhing under the erotic manipulation of his hands, his mouth. With an almost drugged look in his dark eyes, Jake nipped the inside of her thigh and then eased his full length in place over her.

At the slightest touch of his leg against hers Lee opened herself to him, into the mysterious secrets of her womanhood.

Their journey was swift, the course strewn with incoherent words of love, hurled in the spacelessness of time that precedes the climactic explosion. When the cataclysmic eruption came, it left them sated . . . replete.

Long after their breathing had returned to normal, and awareness slowly awakened their bodies to the more mundane senses of touching, seeing, and hearing, Jake smiled lazily down at Lee, snuggled in the protective curve of his arm. "Welcome home, my darling. Welcome home."